THE GIRL WHO WAS TARGETED

ADELINA THRILLER 2

BOOK 2

KATHLEEN GUIRE

CHAPTER
ONE

THE REUNION

My phone vibrated. I picked it up and read the text.

Cecylia: We're coming to West Virginia!

Me: What? When?

I had been *home* with Marge and Jim for seven months. Most of the time, I refer to them as Mom and Dad now. I had been wishing Cecylia would visit. Now she was coming. Cecylia and I hadn't seen each other since we said goodbye at the Chicago airport when we arrived in the United States. This was after we took down Ryszard, Cecylia's step-father, and his human trafficking ring in Poland. I was so glad Cecylia and her mom had come to the states to start a new life.

Cecylia: Tomorrow!

Me: Staying here?

Cecylia: No. Mom had the staff book a
hotel. Spoiler alert - meeting with a
realtor.

Me: You're staying for good?

Cecylia: Maybe. Fill you in tomorrow.

Finally, they were coming here.

"MOM! Cecylia's coming!" I yelled out the open window in the library. Marge was weeding her flower garden in the front, and Jim had gone to get some mulch.

"Come out and tell me about it," she said, still pulling weeds.

I walked out the front door and plopped down on a wicker loveseat. I was reading the texts to her when a large black SUV pulled up in front of the house.

"This is strange," Marge said. She stood and pulled her garden gloves off.

Marge loved her privacy. I had learned she was an introvert. Marge and Jim had bought this place, the home and property, at the end of a neighborhood because Marge needed the seclusion it offered. The home, on seven and a half acres, was so well hidden that most people had a hard time finding it, including the UPS man. Marge used Amazon Prime a lot. You would think the UPS man would get it right, eventually. Amazon saved her the trouble of going out, she said. One click is all it took. Still, we were five to ten minutes away from restaurants, shopping, church and the home-school co-op. Sometimes the house seemed like a giant revolving door with older sister Laura coming with her littles (which made me miss mine). Robert loved to host bonfires with his friends. The music was loud and the S'mores sweet. He let me hang out with his friends until about ten pm, which is when Jim came looking for me. That was enough time for me, anyway. An hour.

Watching Marge helped me discover a lot about myself. I needed time alone to sort things out. I relished time alone. When the dust settled after the bustle of activity, Mom went to her office to write and I settled in the library. A real library with a round, dark walnut table that sat on a large pedestal with ornately carved lions at the bottom. It had lived in a monastery at one time. Fitting, I thought, to remind me of the monastery turned hotel in Sulejow that Marge and Jim had stayed at when they came to adopt me. This library table sat in someone's basement for thirty years before Mom bought and refinished it. The best thing about the library? It had books. Entire books. No one tore out pages and made cigarettes to smoke. No one smoked here, which was weird. Everyone in Poland smoked. I spent hours pouring over books I had wanted to finish at the orphanage. Of course, people interrupted me just as they did in the orphanage. Now it was siblings, not fellow orphans. Robert said, "Adelina, you don't have to read all the books in the library your first year here."

Jim defended me. Marge too. "She's catching up," she'd say, and then she'd smile.

The SUV rolled to a stop and the driver's side window opened.

"Adelina?" a square face, suited man asked. Before Mom or I could say a word, the rear passenger side door opened and Kasia popped out.

"HEY!" she yelled, running toward me across the green lawn. "You're never going to guess what happened!"

Before she could tell us, another door opened and Sabilia stepped down. Her blonde, silky smooth hair grazed her shoulders, and she wore a form-fitted mint-green sleeveless dress, and heels.

"Adelina!" Despite the heels, she ran to the porch and bounded up the stairs. She wrapped her arms around me and gave me a tight squeeze.

"Marge, hi, sorry to stop by unannounced."

Marge laughed. "It's great to see you, Sabilia. 'Stopped unannounced' is a bit of an understatement, isn't it?"

"Yes," she laughed. "I guess you're right." She squeezed me once more and then let me go.

Kasia joined us on the porch. She scanned the yard. "Where's the pool? Can we swim?"

I grabbed her hand and pulled her toward me into a giant bear hug. "You have no idea how much I've been missing you!"

I hadn't seen Sabilia since my surprise party in Poland.

———

Director Josef had checked me out of the hospital. I had recovered enough from my knife wound in the altercation with Ryszard to return to the orphanage.

"Surprise!" The lights came on and brightly colored confetti flew at my face. I tried to take it all in. Jim and

Marge had rushed forward and enveloped me in an embrace.

"We're so glad you're okay, honey." Marge said. Tears dripped down her pink cheeks.

"And we're darn proud of you," Jim added with a catch in his throat.

Sabilia hovered beside them. "You did a great job. A real spy."

Father Raphael stepped in front of me. Marge and Jim stood beside me, protective as guard dogs. "God answered my prayer and kept you safe," he said.

Sabilia and Father Raphael had told me their story. They were siblings! Who knew? The comments at her townhouse about "remember last time" were a tiny piece of the puzzle. Their younger sister, Aneta, had fallen prey to Ryszard. She just wanted to go out and have a good time. Although Father Raphael wouldn't admit it, she had probably confessed to him she was seeing someone older, the same storyline as Daria. The confusing part for the priest and Sabilia was that Aneta wanted for nothing. Her family were aristocrats who had held onto their status and money. Their estate was one of the 20,000 damaged and/or occupied during World War II. Because of their grandfather's wise moves pre-war and a lengthy reconstruction project in the early nineties, all three siblings grew up in the manor.

"I followed Ryszard one night after Aneta disappeared," Father Raphael had said. "I wasn't sure he was the man who had kidnapped Aneta. I was just following my gut, following the bread trails, and acting on her confession. He went to an old abandoned building on the outskirts of Warsaw. I followed him into the building. He didn't hear me until I saw the girls chained to beds. I must have gasped." That's when Ryszard had attacked the priest, slashing his face with the knife. Father Raphael regained consciousness and realized he was alone in the building. They never saw or heard from Aneta again.

———

"Let me make some coffee," Mom said, waking me from my retrospection, "then we can talk. I made some muffins. Give me a minute."

Retrospection-the action, process, or faculty of looking back on things past.

"I'll help." Sabilia followed her in the house while I stayed outside with Kasia.

"You know where the pool is, Kasia, remember? You can tell me what's going on!"

"I know. I've just never seen it uncovered. It was winter last time I was here…….WOW!" she said as she rounded the corner. She stopped. "It's huge. It's so blue. Can I get in?"

"Focus, Kasia, why are you here?"

———

Marge and Jim had found a host family for Kasia. She had traveled to the U.S. with us on the same plane as Cecylia, her mother, and their bodyguards.

In December, Kasia had spent a month with her host family not far from us. It hadn't quite worked out the way we planned. Marge took me to see Kasia once a week, although she hadn't been permitted to visit us. During those visits, the host Mom and Marge drank coffee in the kitchen and the host Mom poured out her woes.

"She's a little too high needs for our family," I overheard. I had guided Kasia into the basement family room. Kasia didn't need to hear her faults listed in front of her. Instead, we played Wii bowling.

On Christmas Eve, Marge, Jim, Robert, Anne and I took Kasia some gifts. Laura had stayed at the house with Lucy and Ivan, my niece and nephew. They were busy making Christmas cookies. Kasia's face lit up with joy when she saw us. "I don't like it here," she cried on my shoulder while I held her on my lap. "They don't like me."

She had opened her gifts and cheered up. Marge had bought her a hoodie with a giant heart. Jim had picked out a charm bracelet with a heart. He was such a softy sometimes. I had heard Robert say that. I wasn't sure what it meant until Jim stopped at the jewelry store in the mall during our Christmas shopping trip.

"Jim, she's eight years old. What are you going to buy her?" Marge had asked.

"Every little girl needs jewelry." He winked at me and bought the charm bracelet. He also bought Mom a ring and asked my opinion about it before he shoved me out of the store. The stone looked orange, like a pumpkin. It matched Mom's hair, so I said, "yes, that one." I knew nothing about jewelry.

Mom, Anne and I had bought the hoodie, some jeans and tennis shoes. I also had to buy her a book, *The*

Secret Garden. Anne had suggested I read it and I loved it. I thought Kasia would too. I planned to read it to her.

It was Christmas Eve when the host mom had told us that Kasia was going back to the orphanage for good.

"We're having my family over tomorrow. All of my siblings and their children. We will have a full house." She looked at me as if I understood what she was saying. Her mouth turned down in a frown. I had thought she was beautiful in the beginning. Long dark hair the color of chestnuts and amber-colored eyes. She reminded me of a character in a fairytale. I had first thought her a princess. Now, I thought her a witch.

Robert had pulled Dad aside in the entryway. I followed.

"Dad, do something. Are you going to let this witch get away with it? With hurting Kasia?"Robert said. His face was red and fists clenched. "I'm going to the car!"

This had made me feel better. I wasn't the only one who saw the host mom as a princess turned evil witch. From the foyer, I heard Mom say, "Why doesn't Kasia spend the day with us then?" Robert stopped, his hand on the door knob. He looked at Dad.

"Oh, could she?" Host Mom replied.

"Of course," Jim had said and in two steps, he was back in the kitchen. Robert right beside him, matching his steps. Dad cleared his throat, "let's pack her up now. She can spend the night."

So Kasia had spent the last few days of her visit with us. We played games, sang songs, ate tons of cookies, and Kasia played with Lucy and Ivan. Laura's husband Daniel joined us for Christmas day before getting on a plane for another business trip. Laura and the kids stayed with us for days after, making the house lively and fun. The whole Hunter family had taken Kasia to the airport and seen her off. A bubbly flight attendant had taken charge of her at the gate. We all shed tears. Kasia had clung to me.

"I can't lose you!" she sobbed.

In January, Mom and Dad started the paperwork to adopt her, only to find out that someone else had already initiated the process and gotten approved. We had heard nothing since.

———

Kasia peeled her sandals off and dipped her foot in the pool.

"It feels great!"

I ran down the bank toward the pool. "Did Sabilia adopt you?"

"Yep!" she said, stepping down until the water covered her knees. "That's what I was trying to tell you!"

"Girls, come up here!" It was Marge. She and Sabilia were on the deck, muffins, and coffee in hand.

"I want to swim!" Kasia said, stepping out of the pool.

"After we talk and you get settled," Marge answered.

"You're staying? They're staying?" Kasia was too busy stomping up the stairs to answer me.

"Yes," for a few days Sabilia said, and she handed me a coffee.

Just like old times, I thought. *Those days in the*

orphanage seemed like a lifetime ago. I loved the way Sabilia treated me. Like a human. My new family treated me the same. My coping mechanism (Marge's name for it) had died down quite a bit. I still memorized poetry and sometimes it popped in my head when it applied to a situation, but I didn't have to recite it as often to calm myself. Same with my dictionary habits. The first day of homeschool co-op was horrific. All I did was define words and recite poetry. In the middle of class once, I answered with a verse. Talk about mortification.

Mortify-to subject to severe and vexing embarrassment : shame

Just thinking about it sent me into my old habits. This situation with Sabilia wasn't helping. Why was she here? What was going on?

I sat down, gripping my coffee with both hands, so as not to spill it.

"We need your help, Adelina. We followed all the leads we had from Ryszard and the organization. The last lead led us here."

"What?" I stood up and my coffee cup hit the deck. Coffee spread out on the deck while the fiestaware cup bounced in slow motion.

"To West Virginia?" Marge said, as she stood and put her arm around my shoulders. I watched the coffee spread and drip through the cracks wastefully spilling my new found felt-safety.

spill-to cause or allow to run or fall from a container, especially accidentally or wastefully:

"Yes, we've taken down some other rings in other countries. Some of these girls end up back on the street. I'll get into that later. One of our contacts here in the states said she had spotted Ryszard."

Marge and I sat down at the same time.

Robert opened the back door and stuck his head out. "What's going on, Mom? Adelina, are you okay?"

He disappeared and reappeared with a pitcher of water which he poured on the coffee puddle. It streamed through cracks on the deck to the patio below. He picked up the coffee mug and sat down beside me.

He stuck his hand out to Sabilia. "I'm Robert."

Kasia flung herself on his lap. "I want to go swimming, Robert!"

Just then, we heard the truck being driven into the front yard. Jim was back with the mulch.

"I'll go fill Jim in," Marge said as she stood. "Adelina, will you be okay?"

"I'm here, Mom. I've got this. Go talk to dad," Robert said. "Kasia, go put your suit on."

Kasia bounded into the house, slamming the door behind her.

"If Ryszard is here, why do you need my help?" I could finally formulate a sentence.

"He may have set up a ring in this area and he may be looking for you. We're not sure. If he is looking for you, we need to protect you."

"But you said you need my help. So, you mean use me as bait again?"

"Oh no you don't," Robert said, raising to his full height. "That didn't work out so well the last time."

Kasia was back, swinging her towel around. "I'm ready!"

"Adelina, why don't you take Kasia down to the pool while we finish this discussion?"

Robert looked so much like Jim right then. He

shooed me down the stairs to the pool. Kasia was right behind me. As soon as we were on the pool patio, Kasia threw her towel down and jumped in. She bobbed back up, squealing.

"It's perfect!" she yelled.

I sat down in a chair to watch her. I glanced up at the deck where Jim, Marge, Robert, and Sabilia were now talking. I couldn't make out exactly what they were saying. The filter and air conditioner drowned them out.

"It won't be the same," Sabilia said. Jim answered. I couldn't hear the words. I recognized the posture. He would not budge. No, I would not be helping this time. I turned my attention to Kasia.

"Where do you live, Kasia?"

"What? We're moving here for a while. Father Raphael, Sabilia, and I are looking at some houses tomorrow."

Hmmm. Cecylia was coming. Moving here. Sabilia moving here. Sounds like someone already had a plan in place.

Anne joined us at the pool. "Robert said for me to monitor you." She pushed my shoulder with her hand, "you okay?"

"I'm fine," I lied. She had her suit on. The orange swimsuit matched her red hair. We could be sisters. Oh wait, we were sisters.

"Go get your suit on. I'll watch her for a few minutes."

"Anne eeeeee, get in!" Kasia yelled. Anne ran to the side and did a cannonball, splashing me, and Kasia squealed again.

I ran up the stairs, went inside, and changed into my swimsuit. Anne, Kasia, and I spent the next hour playing in the pool. It felt good to get my mind off of the reason Sabilia was here. Anne didn't mention it. We dove for the swim rings and played tag. Anne is good at distracting me. At cheering me up. It wasn't until right before lunch that it hit me.

I was in my room sliding back into my shorts and I saw his face. His evil grin. As I looked at the purple scar on my arm where Ryszard had stabbed me, fear washed over me. I stood up. Poetry sped through my mind like Flash. My mind couldn't settle on a poem. The words mixed like poetry in a blender. Anne poked her head in the door. "Lunch is ready. Adelina, sit down!"

She rushed over and took my arm. "Tell me about it."

"I just keep seeing his face."

"Ryszard's?"

"Yeah."

"Are you doing that poetry thing again? Maybe if you recite something, it will help."

"I can't. It's all a jumble."

"Adelina, *you* are the reason he was captured him the first time."

I took a few deep breaths. "I know you're right. My body just doesn't want to cooperate."

"Then, do it afraid. I'm here. I can help. Robert's here. Laura. Daniel. Mom. Dad."

"I'm here," Kasia stuck her head in the door. "And it's time to eat. Marge said."

We went down the steps together. Everyone was in

the kitchen. Robert and Dad were making sandwiches while Mom served fruit salad.

"I want to help, Sabilia. I want to take Ryszard down for good."I said.

"Great!" Sabilia said. "We have a task force here in West Virginia. We'll take you to our headquarters and get you settled in."

"No!" I said a little too quickly. "I'm not going to a headquarters or whatever you have set up." I looked around the kitchen at my family."This is my headquarters. This is my task force."

"Yeah," Robert said, flinging his sandwich onto his plate. "We're her task force. Mom? Dad?"

"Yep!" they both said in unison.

"She's not going into the lion's den alone this time," Jim said.

"Cecylia is part of our task force too!" I said, remembering the text. "She's coming tomorrow!"

We settled into lunch, everyone talking at once. It was like old times.

"This is the most unorthodox task force ever," Sabilia said and slumped back in her chair.

Kasia, Sabilia, her brother the priest, my former enemy and now friend, Cecylia, and my new family.

I smiled. It is the best task force ever.

Sabilia's phone buzzed. "A text from my brother," she said, explaining. She stood waving her phone around in the air like a flag.

"Aneta is alive! My sister is alive! One of the task force members sighted her here in the states!" she read.

THE RESPITE and Renewal

Summer was winding down. There was no fresh news about Aneta. Sabilia and Kasia had rented a townhouse right over the hill from us in the same neighborhood that Cecylia and her mother had purchased a home. Cecylia's mother had whittled their staff down to a minimum so as not to stick out like a sore thumb, a phrase I had overheard Mom saying about Amelia and her entourage. The body guards were still around, but a little more inconspicuous and wearing regular clothes.

Cecylia, Kasia, and I had spent many summer days together swimming in the pool, hiking in the woods and just goofing off. It was weird and normal all at the same time.

nor·mal-

conforming to a standard; usual, typical, or expected.

I still defined words when I was super nervous. The excitement at the beginning of the summer. The

Aneta sighting. Ryszard in the states. A new Task Force. These all seemed to fade into the background, and I liked it that way. I still had my moments, though.

Mom, Rob, and I were starting school this week. Sabilia decided to homeschool Kasia too. We would all be attending the same homeschool co-op. It felt like family; I think. Mom had enrolled Rob and me in a course at Red Maple University, so we could "get our feet wet," she said. Cecylia enrolled in RMU as a full-time student. She had grand plans for wardrobe shopping with me.

I leaned back into the leather library chair and watched the first few leaves swirl around and fall off the trees. *This is going to be a great school year.* I wrote in my journal. Anne had given the journal to me for my birthday. She told me to write about the thoughts that bugged me. I filled the first half of it with poetry and definitions. Now, I seem to find some positive thoughts to write about, once in a while.

A loud rap on the window startled me and I jumped out of the chair, falling forward and catching myself on the edge of the library table. I turned and Rob had his face smashed up against the glass. I laughed. It felt good to laugh.

"Get out here! I have the fire started! Bring the hotdogs!"

I ran upstairs to put my journal away and then joined Mom in the kitchen. Minutes later, Mom and I packed hot dogs, chips, and condiments in baskets and headed outside. A bunch of Rob's friends lounged around the firepit in the Adirondack chairs, talking and laughing. Sabilia pulled up in her SUV and Kasia hopped out.

"Where are the hotdog sticks?" she yelled as she ran straight for the fire.

Rob grabbed her and swung her away from the flames. "Woah, Nelly! Take a seat. Not too close."

Sabilia walked toward Mom and the picnic table. I joined them.

"The trail just seems dead." Sabilia's shoulders slumped forward as she said it.

"I'm sorry," Marge said.

"What trail?" And there was Cecylia, appearing out of nowhere, as usual.

"Aneta's," Mom said.

"Oh," Cecylia said, making a small o with her lips. "So..hey, Mom and I rode our bikes over. Can you believe it? Mom, on a bike!"

Just then, Amelia peddled up, flanked by two bulky body guards. True to form, she wore all pink, although it was spandex.

"This is where the party is?" She said with a laugh. She sounded just like Cecylia.

I joined Kasia and Rob at the firepit. He was helping her roast a hot dog.

"Hello, my name is Irfan," said a voice to the left of me.

I turned to see warm chocolate eyes and a handsome dark complexion. He startled me, both with his introduction and his handsome features. Why did I keep thinking handsome?

Handsome- good looking.

Get your head together, girl! My mind was going a

million miles a minute. I could feel a poem coming on. Don't say it out loud. Don't say it out loud.

"Why do I love" You, Sir?
Because—
The Wind does not require the Grass
To answer—Wherefore when He pass
She cannot keep Her place.
Because He knows—and
Do not You—
And We know not—
Enough for Us
The Wisdom it be so—[1]

"The wind…" I started and stopped.

I could feel the flames rising up my neck. My face was on fire. Just then, the wind picked up and blew smoke in my face. Thank you, God.

"Yeah," Rob interjected. "The wind is picking up. You should scoot over, Adelina."

Saved by the wind, God, and my new brother. I didn't know how to talk to people in general (except family and I still struggled with that). Cute guys were a whole other species. Like aliens.

Rob grabbed my chair and moved it to the other side of the fire pit. Irfan followed. Really? He's following me? Should I run in the house? I didn't have a great track record with guys. They made me false promises. One of them lost his golden locks to my scissor hands. The other one, I stabbed, and he was here in the states looking for me.

"Oh, hey Irfan, this is my sister, Adelina." Rob said.

"Adelina, this is Irfan. We met at one of those RMU

welcome days you didn't want to attend." He jabbed me with his elbow and laughed.

I wasn't sure what was so funny. I didn't want to go to the *Welcome to RMU Day*. I just wanted the art class to start so I could learn more. I didn't think I cared who was in the class.

"Are you taking Art 101?" I attempted a smile. It felt more like a grimace, but I was trying.

"I took that last year," he smiled, and I felt warm in the pit of my stomach. Maybe I was getting the flu. I would ask Mom later. I never got this feeling from the teen boys in the orphanage.

"I'm taking 102," he added while I tried to think of something coherent to say.

"Oh, nice," I said. I looked at the fire instead of him. That helped.

"Are you an artist?" he asked.

"I want to be." I said quietly.

"Don't listen to her. She is talented." Cecylia said from behind me. She grabbed a chair and scooted in between us.

"Hi," she said as she flipped her hair. "I'm Cecylia."

"Hi. We met, remember? At your orientation." Irfan said.

"Oh, I wasn't sure if you remembered me." She giggled.

"How could I forget?" he said. Was that irritation in his voice? Or was I imagining it?

Irfan leaned forward and angled his head toward me. "Tell me more about your art."

Cecylia jumped up and said, "Well, I must move on and mingle with someone who appreciates me."

Irfan laughed. I didn't know that was a joke. Was it?

I spent the next fifteen minutes listening to Irfan talk about art. Once in a while I nodded or said, "yeah." That's about all I could muster. Definitions and poetry flitted through my head the whole time. I tried to stuff them down into the deep recesses of my mind. I'll write this all out in my journal later. I told myself.

"Okay. Okay. Move on, Irfan. You've grilled Adelina enough," Rob said, as he pulled Irfan up by the elbow. "Adelina, Sabilia needs to talk to you inside now."

Irfan shook his arm away and moved toward a group of guys putting marshmallows on sticks. "Fine. I'm going to make a S'more. Catch you later, Adelina!"

I went in the front door, looking for Sabilia. She was sitting at the library table sipping coffee with Mom.

"I see you found the mark," she said casually. "Good work."

The mark? Good work? What was she talking about?

"What?!" I was confused.

"Irfan."

Once again, my illusions popped like a giant pink balloon.

"Cecylia tried to get close to him. She just couldn't make a connection."

"You think he's linked to Ryszard?" I plopped down into a chair a little too hard. The blood rose to my cheeks.

"We're not sure. That's what we need you to find out. Rob tried getting him to open up. Nothing."

"And why do you think he'll open up to me?"

"We saw him out there talking to you. His body language says he likes you."

Dang. What did my body language say?

"Why do I love" You, Sir?
Because—
The Wind does not require the Grass
To answer—Wherefore when He pass
She cannot keep Her place.[2]
Stop it! Focus.

"Do you think he is a scout?" I asked.

"We don't really know anything, do we, Sabilia? He might just be a nice kid. Right?"

"Right. You're right, Marge. I may just be over reacting," Sabilia said. "I think I'm just grasping at straws. I want to find Aneta." She put her face in her hands and wept. Marge patted her on the back.

"I don't like this." I said. "This feels like Poland all over again. Are all my friends spies or scouts or something?"

Mom reached over and put my hand on my shoulder. "You don't have to do this," she said.

"He may be our only lead," Sabilia sobbed.

"He may be no lead at all." Marge countered. "You can't brand every foreign exchange student a scout or terrorist."

"I know. I know." Sabilia wiped her eyes with a tissue Marge handed her.

"I want to talk to Father Raphael before I decide." I said. "Also, I want to enjoy Rob's back to school bonfire. I'm going out to make a S'more with Kasia and plan a shopping day with Cecylia. Like normal people do. *I think.*" The last sentence kind of trailed off in a wave of doubt.

"I'll get my brother on the phone right away," Sabilia said, her face brightening.

"No. Not tonight and not on the phone. In person." I said, more forcefully than intended.

The front door swung open and Anne stepped in, pulling off a Starbucks apron in one motion. She took one look at the three of us and said, "What's going on? Did you find Ryszard? Aneta? What?"

"No to all the above," Mom said.

"Sabilia wants me to spy again. Same old stuff." I laughed when I said it. Was this my new crazy normal? Make a friend. Spy on friend.

"Oh." she said. "I'm going out there to make a hot dog and a S'more. Work was a killer." I guess it was her new normal, too.

Anne changed, and we went out to the fire together. Kasia was dancing around the fire, a bit out of control. Anne grabbed her and pulled her back to safety.

"Hey, help me make a hot dog!" she said. That kept Kasia occupied and safe for a few minutes while I went looking for Cecylia.

She was standing by the S'more stuff, eating a chocolate bar.

"Cecylia, when are we going back to school shopping?"

"OOOOOOO. I thought you'd never ask! I'll ask Mom if we can use the car and the driver."

Shopping with Cecylia was a three-ring circus. We had a car, a driver, and bodyguards. It was worth it, though. I felt safer, in case Ryszard was lurking around the shopping mall looking for us.

"Want to go tomorrow?" I asked. "We only have a week before classes start."

"Yep! Let's make a list." She pulled out her phone and opened a notes app.

I did the same. Getting accustomed to technology was a challenge for me. I was learning. We spent the next twenty minutes looking at clothing and accessories online and making a list. We found two seats near the fire and continued our pre-shopping.

"We definitely need boots and sweaters. Cute ones!" She said as she added them to the list. "Maybe a wool poncho?"

"What's up girls? You disappeared, Adelina." Irfan said, leaning over my shoulder.

"Just had stuff to do." I said quietly.

"Oh." he said as he sat down beside me.

His phone glowed. I looked at the screen. He did too. A text came through with a small photo beside it. He looked up and shut the screen down. It went black, but not before I saw the text and the photo. It was Aneta.

Are you at the bonfire? Did you see her?

I gagged as if I was going to vomit. Cecylia reacted quickly, patting my back and handing me a water bottle.

Thou blind fool, Love, what dost thou to mine eyes,
That they behold and see not what they see?
They know what beauty is, see where it lies,
Yet what the best is take the worst to be.
If eyes, corrupt by over-partial looks,

Be anchored in the bay where all men ride,
Why of eyes' falsehood hast thou forgèd hooks,
Whereto the judgment of my heart is tied?[3]

"Breathe girl. He's cute, but he's not worth dying over," Cecylia whispered. There was no need to whisper. Irfan didn't hear her. He hurried to his car, hopped in, and sped away.

Wait. What was going on? Why was he texting Aneta? Was she part of the whole human trafficking thing? That would kill Sabilia and Father Raphael. Should I tell them what I saw?

"Did you see that?" I asked Cecylia after I chugged some water. My voice was hoarse and raspy. I could still feel the bile in my throat.

"What? You spying on your new boyfriend's texts or him leaving in a rush? What did you say to him? I know he's the mark. You don't have to pretend with me."

"Yeah, right? That makes me feel secure."

"Are you being sarcastic? Don't Adelina. It doesn't suit you. I didn't see who was texting him. Did you?"

I forgave Cecylia. I did. There were just some moments she rubbed me the wrong way.

"No, I saw nothing." I lied. "I just still get nervous about this stuff."

"Don't worry. I've got your back," she patted me on the back.

Then I felt bad. What should I do with the information?

I needed to talk to the priest.

CHAPTER
THREE

THE RATIFICATION

"You wanted to see me?" Father Raphael sat on the family room couch sipping coffee.

I rubbed the sleep from my eyes and walked to the Keurig. I grabbed a mug from the cupboard and a pod from the carousel.

I needed to think. I was stalling. Why did he come so early? What d0 I tell him? Aneta is still alive, but she's working for the other side? She's hunting for me and using my brother's friends. No, I couldn't tell him that. I turned and smiled at him, a crooked smile. It wasn't an actual smile. He could tell. He was on his feet and in three long strides, he was beside me. He opened the fridge and pulled out the coconut milk. He knew me so well. That's what made this so hard. I liked it better when he couldn't read me. Now, he came for Sunday dinners and cookouts like he was part of the family. Yikes.

I took the coconut milk and scooped some of the fat into my coffee and stirred it. *Stalling.*

Stall- stop or cause to stop making progress.

"Hey, are you stalling?" He said with a grin.

"What? NO. I just need some coffee first. I mean. YES." I walked over to Mom's chair and sat down. "Hey, where is everyone?"

"Stalling. Stalling. Stalling," he said and snapped his hands and shook his hips.

Was that a dance? Stop it. Just stop it. Why was he in such a good mood? I'm about to crush his dream. His mood.

Rob sauntered into the room and sat in dad's chair. "Is this a private meeting? I didn't get a memo. Oh coffee. I want some!"

He jumped up and headed to the Keurig.

Father Raphael snapped his fingers again. His hips gyrated in a weird back-and-forth motion.

"Father, what is that?" Rob had turned towards us while his coffee brewed. "Stop. Just stop. For the love of God and all that is holy."

"Sorry, I'm just in a good mood. Plus, I watched this show. Dancing with the Stars?"

"Well, don't. Whatever you're doing."

"Yes." Father said.

"Yes, you'll stop?"

"Yes, this is a private meeting."

"Oh. Well, in that case, I'm outta here." He stomped down the hallway and up the steps to his room, and slammed the door. I noticed Rob didn't take not being "in the know as" Dad called it, very well. Neither did dad. He likes to be in charge. In control.

We sat down. I was hoping for another stalling technique to come to mind. I couldn't think of one.

"The thing is, Father, I told Sabilia I wouldn't help with this latest person, thing, project, unless I talked to you."

"Right. Right." He took his large hands and placed them on his knees. "I'm here."

Why did he look so durn happy?

"Well, that was before I found out another piece of information. I'm not sure talking to you will help now. I've decided to sit this one out."

"I see." He rubbed his temple with his fingers, in tiny circles.

"We all want progress, but if you're on the wrong road, progress means doing an about-turn and walking back to the right road; in that case, the man who turns back soonest is the most progressive,"

[1] I said quietly.

"You're quoting C.S. Lewis to ME?"

"Yes, I am making progress. I used to only quote things in my head. It's how I process things."

"So, this new information. You're not sharing?" He stood. He wasn't dancing anymore. He ran his hands through his hair and it stood on end. From happy to crazed looking. And it was all my fault.

"I'm turning away from this one, Father. You have an entire team at your disposal."

I stood too. I walked to the sink and dumped out the remainder of my coffee. I was too jittery to drink the rest. I wasn't going to be the one who told him his sister had turned. Add her to the list of people trying to kill me.

"I'm going to take a walk in the woods. Want to join me?" I said, changing the subject.

"Really?"

"Yes, on one condition. We don't talk about this case. Ryszard. Irfan or any of it."

"Deal." He said. " I could use some fresh air."

"Let me get changed," I said. "I'll be right back."

What has changed my mind? Last night, I thought if I talked to Father Raphael that everything would be okay. As soon as my head hit the pillow, I knew it wasn't so. All night I tossed and turned, walking through every scenario. None of them came out pretty. None of them were yellow.

> Two roads diverged in a yellow wood,
> And sorry I could not travel both
> And be one traveler, long I stood
> And looked down one as far as I could
> To where it bent in the undergrowth;[2]

Both of them were full of undergrowth. I rummaged in my drawer for some yoga pants and a t-shirt. I pulled out a gray v-neck.

"Hey, Adelina, what are you doing in there?" Rob leaned all of his weight on the door and jiggled the handle.

"I'm changing. Rob, don't come in!"

"Okay. Okay. Don't have a cow. Mom told me to keep an eye on you while she was at the store."

"Have a cow? I don't even know what that means. I don't need a sitter."

"Listen, I'm just following orders. Don't shoot the messenger."

"What? You're weird. You talk weird too," I said as I opened the door and shoved him out of the way. "I'm going for a walk in the woods with Father Raphael."

"You're weird and I'm coming."

I ran down the stairs with Rob two inches behind me.

Gosh.

Father Raphael stood at the door, his hand on the door knob. "Are you both coming?"

"Yes, Rob wants to make sure I don't have any cows or shoot messengers."

We all three sloshed along in the leaves that already carpeted the forest floor. It reminded me of the woods between the village and the orphanage back in Poland.

A yellow leaf danced in the air in front of me.

"Two roads diverged in a yellow wood,

And sorry I could not travel both

And be one traveler, long I stood

And looked down one as far as I could

"To where it bent in the undergrowth;[3]" Father recited.

"You too?" I said, amazed. I stopped and looked at him with new wonder.

"Then took the other, as just as fair,

And having perhaps the better claim,

Because it was grassy and wanted wear;

Though as for that the passing there"[4]

"Had worn them really about the same," Rob added. "Yes, Adelina, other people recite poetry. It's not just your weirdo habit.

I laughed. *We* all laughed and recited the last two stanzas together.

"And both that morning equally lay
In leaves no step had trodden black.
Oh, I kept the first for another day!
Yet knowing how way leads on to way,
I doubted if I should ever come back.
I shall be telling this with a sigh
Somewhere ages and ages hence:
Two roads diverged in a wood, and I—
I took the one less traveled by,
And that has made all the difference."[5]

Rob leaned back and picked up a pile of leaves and threw them my way. I followed suit and so did Father. We were running around laughing. I had leaves in my hair. So did everyone else. It smelled like heaven.

And then the second thoughts hit. Should I take the road less traveled? The one with truth and tell Father. As quickly as the thoughts came, they left. I was having too much fun. Rob might be a pain and think I gave birth to cows, but he knew how to make me laugh. I guess that's what brothers were supposed to be like.

Rob shoved me to the ground and held my head down. I tried to scream. I couldn't see Father.

"Shhhhhh," he whispered. "Someone followed us."

I held still. My heart thumping in my chest. I should have told the truth. It had to be Aneta or Ryszard. Or Irfan? Here to finish me. Poor Father. Probably him too.

I heard rustling in the trees. Leaves crackled and crunched loudly. Rob had let go of my head and I turned it sideways. I saw boots running toward me. I raised my head just a bit. A torso was connected to legs, which were connected to the boots. A torso with Irfan's head on top. Great. So much for not telling Father Raphael. I looked for a weapon. Maybe he didn't see me. I tried to bury myself deeper. I couldn't see Rob or Father.

Irfan opened his mouth and someone or something came out of nowhere and Irfan's slim, lanky body went flying and hit a tree. He landed upside down, his legs sticking up parallel to the trunk. I heard the familiar audible whoosh of air being knocked out of his lungs. He wouldn't be saying anything for a few seconds.

"What are you doing here, Irfan?"

It was Rob. I stood up and dusted the leaf particles from my person, and joined Rob. Father Raphael stepped out of the shadows. He had a handgun. He pointed it at Irfan.

"What?" Irfan said. "No need for guns." He did a somersault down the hill and stood feebly.

"I repeat. What are you doing here?" Rob said as he grabbed my arm and shoved me behind him.

"I was looking for Adelina."

"That's what we thought," Father said, looking larger, taller and scary.

"You're here to kill me, right?" I stuck my head out from behind Rob's back. "You're here because Aneta sent you."

Rob and Father's heads swiveled towards me in synchronized movement.

All three of them said, "What?" at the same time.

"Aneta. She sent you. I wanted to tell you Father Raphael, I did. But, you were so happy. We were so glad to have news of her sighting. Then last night I found out she's on the other side. She's one of them." I pointed at Irfan.

"One of us? What do you mean? Who do you mean? A foreign exchange student. Yes, that's how I met her."

"This is getting so confusing," Rob said.

"You're telling me," Irfan said. "Could you please just lower the gun? Aren't you a priest? Are you supposed to have one of those?"

"Frisk him, Adelina." Father Raphael said.

My face flushed hot. "I'm not frisking him. He's a …. Well, a …."

"Go ahead, say it," Irfan said. "A terrorist. That's what you guys think, huh? That's what this is all about. Man, my dad said this would happen. Don't go to America, he said, they'll call you a terrorist because you're Middle Eastern." He walked in small circles, kicking up leaves with both hands on his head like a criminal.

"Guy." I said loudly, "because you're a GUY."

Now, his face was red. "You do it, Rob," Father said.

Rob walked over and patted him down. "He's clean. Cool, I always wanted to say that."

Father Raphael put the gun back in the holster. "Let's take a seat and sort this out."

He found a log and sat down. He patted the log, and we all joined him.

"Who are you people?" Irfan said.

"NO. NO. NO!" I said just a little too loudly, again. "The question is- who are YOU? Why are you here?"

"I told you. I'm Irfan. I'm not a terrorist. Just a kid trying to get an education."

"What she means is, what did you come to tell us?"

"Not until you tell me why a priest has a gun."

We sat for a few minutes in silence. Great. The priest and his vow of silence thing again. Rob only knew what Mom and Dad had told him. I didn't know if he knew all of it.

"Okay. Okay." I said. I stood up. He wasn't here to kill me or he would have done it already. How much did I tell? I jumped back and forth over the log reciting in my head.

I shall be telling this with a sigh
Somewhere ages and ages hence:
Two roads diverged in a wood, and I—
I took the one less traveled by,
And that has made all the difference.
"I shall be telling this with a sigh…"[6]

"What?" Irfan said.

"Be quiet," Rob said. "She's warming up."

A large branch crackled on a tree behind me. It fell. I hit the dirt. The leaves rustled. Was this a set up? Did Irfan come here as a distraction so the real killer could strike?

"What's going on? You okay, Adelina? From under the leaf cover, I peered out and spotted a pink converse and two pairs of Nikes. Cecylia. It was time I stopped wondering how she just appeared out of nowhere at the oddest times. I don't know why I still found it surprising.

I stood. *Again.* And dusted myself off.

"What are you doing?" I asked.

"Jogging," she said. "Mom won't let me go alone. I have to take Frick and Frack here." If the bodyguards were annoyed, they didn't show it. Cecylia sat down on the log. "A meeting in the woods. How secretive and mysterious. I love it."

Irfan twitched. His arms flew up in the air, "I repeat. Who are you people?"

"What's up with him?" Cecylia said, smoothing her pink track pants.

The bodyguards moved toward Irfan. "Calm down, son. Take a seat," they frisked him. Okay, maybe that was overkill. But they didn't know we had already handled that part. After frisking him, Frick, I mean Rick, dropped Irfan on the ground like a sack of potatoes. Frick and Frack stood guard over him as Irfan curled up in a ball and rocked back and forth. "I want to go home," he whimpered.

"Man up," Rob said as he helped Irfan to his feet. "It's okay Rick and Dan. He's okay. You were saying, "Adelina."

"Okay."I paced back and forth. "Here's the thing. I'm part of a task force that took down a sex trafficking ring in Poland last year. So is the priest. And Cecylia."

"What? What does that have to do with me? And aren't you a teenager?" Irfan stood and started pacing the opposite direction.

"It's a long story. Here's where you come in. A girl texted you last night at the party. Aneta."

"Right, that's what I came to talk to you about."

"Well, she's the priest's little sister. A long time ago, someone kidnapped her and we thought she was dead.

"Wow. Wow. This is crazy. It's like I just dropped into the middle of some crime thriller."

"Focus!" Father Raphael said, "you said you came to tell us something about Aneta. You saw her? Is she okay? Where is she?" Father was on his feet, advancing towards Irfan like he was going to devour him. Irfan took a few steps back and Father Raphael pinned him against a tree with his arm. Irfan stiffened. He looked like the rabbit that got stuck in the fence by the pool. His eyes bulged out.

"Um, she looked pretty good. I mean, not pretty. Healthy." Father pressed harder and Irfan gasped for breath.

"Father, he's just the messenger," Rob said. Father Raphael released him and stepped back.

He looked up toward heaven, made the sign of the cross, and looked back at Irfan. "I'm sorry," he said, and sat back down.

"You are the strangest priest I've ever met," Irfan said as he rubbed his neck. "How did you get that scar anyway?"

"By getting into a fight with Ryszard, the man I stabbed." I was getting impatient and over sharing. I looked towards Rob. Yep, over sharing. It was obvious by his expression, he didn't know the stabbing part of the story.

"Sheesh," he said under his breath. "Maybe you should watch out for me, Adelina."

"Well," I prodded.

"Well, it's kind of personal. I mean, I don't want to tell everyone. I just wanted to tell you, Adelina." He held his neck with both hands and shuffled his feet back and forth.

"Well. You just have to tell us all," Rick said. He moved toward Irfan with a menacing expression.

"I'm calling Sabilia," Father said.

"Who? Wait. No need to call her. Who is she? Like your interrogator?"

"She's his sister," Cecylia said with a giggle. "Get a hold of yourself. We're the good guys."

"Okay, okay, here goes. I like you, Adelina. I do. I don't like the girl who was texting me. I didn't want you to think I rushed out of here because I didn't."

"That's what you came to tell us?"

"No, that's what I came to tell her."

"Oh," I could feel the redness rising up my neck. Was I embarrassed or angry? Both. I think both.

"What about Aneta?" I yelled.

"What about her? I told you I didn't like her."

"I think you're missing the point," Rob said.

"How do you know her?" Cecylia added.

"Why is she texting you?" Father said.

"Oh… I met her at a luncheon for foreign exchange students. We exchanged numbers. It meant nothing," He looked at me when he said the last sentence.

"Why did she say, did you see her? Did you find her?"

"Oh, that, well, you didn't come to the orientation event that Rob came to. Your name was on the list. Aneta was working at the orientation. She's some sort of advisor or RA or something. She found out I was coming to the bonfire and she knew you were Rob's sister. I just thought she was trying to check on you. Like it was her responsibility or something. That's all."

Something was super stinky fishy, but it was obvious Irfan didn't have a clue what was going on.

"I need to get back so mom doesn't have a cow," Cecylia said.

"Everyone's having cows!" I said. We laughed. The tension seemed to dissipate.

"Let's get back to the house and have some lunch," Rob suggested. "You too, Irfan."

"Okay," he said and looked at me. Why was he looking at me? His eyes were all soft and brown and gooey. Stop it. Stop it. Stop it.

"Wait, why did you leave last night?"

"I was nervous. Okay. A pretty girl. A fire. ..."

"Yes, I have that effect on people," Cecylia said as she turned, flipped her hair, and headed down the trail.

We hiked back up the hill to the house. Sabilia had parked her SUV out front. Mom was on the front porch with her. They both had their heads down. Great. Everyone's in on it. I had a sinking feeling I was about to be berated.

Berated-scold or criticize (someone) angrily.

Irfan had no idea what was coming.

Irfan was about to join a task force, whether he liked it.

"Adelina, come here. You have some explaining to do," Mom said. Yep, beeeeee rated.

CHAPTER
FOUR

I stood in the doorway of the Art Education building.

"Go in, Adelina. I can't believe you stabbed a guy but you're afraid to go in the classroom," Rob said, shoving me from behind.

"Would you stop bringing that up? I wish you didn't know that. This is different."

My knees were shaking uncontrollably. It was the first day of class on the RMU campus. Anne had dropped us off at the Coliseum and gone on to class herself. I almost didn't get to come. The berating had turned into a grounding. Mom was super upset I had hidden information from her, dad, Sabilia, and Father Raphael. I didn't get it. We did stuff like that in the orphanage all the time. Sometimes you just hide stuff. It was the way you survived. I was becoming more aware that my choices affected other people, but I was hoping the whole Daria and the sex trafficking thing were just a one-time deal. I didn't know the effects would keep happening. I thought once we got to the states, I could start living my life for me.

"You're grounded," Mom had said. Her face turned beet red. I had never seen her like this.

Anne, who was standing behind me enjoying my beration (is that a word?) laughed.

"What are you laughing at, Anne?" Mom said through gritted teeth.

"No offense, mom, but grounding Adelina isn't a punishment. It's the opposite of that. She is a major homebody like you."

"What's grounded?" I said when everyone got quiet.

"That means you can't go anywhere," Rob volunteered from the dining room where he had been listening in. "I'm just eating a sandwich! I can't help it, I can hear everything you're saying."

"Okay. That sounds good. So, I don't have to go to that class you signed me up for?" I started down the hallway.

"See?" Anne said.

"Wait, Adelina, just wait."

I turned and walked back to the kitchen. This family stuff was strange. Why didn't they just yell, lock me in a closet or something, and get it over with?

"You are going to art class, right mom?" Anne said, grabbing my arm and leading me to a stool at the island. Rob came in and plopped himself down on the other stool.

Mom sighed, "yes, she's going."

"And I'll be with her," Rob said.

"That doesn't make me feel any better," I said. They

all laughed. I wasn't sure what was so funny. I was serious. A nervous chuckle escaped from me. This was the campus where Aneta, who "had turned to the dark side" was hunting for me. That meant Ryszard wasn't far away. He could be in West Virginia right now.

As if mom read my mind she said, "we do not know what is going on with Aneta. She could have escaped. She may be looking for a way in. We don't know."

"Yeah, and she will not grab you and kidnap you in broad daylight," Rob said.

That kid knew nothing. Nothing at all. What were my parents thinking, having him watch over me?

A Death blow is a Life blow to Some
Who till they died, did not alive become —
Who had they lived, had died but when
They died, Vitality begun.[1]

I had almost died. Now, I wanted to live, not be in constant fear for my life. As much as I enjoyed having Rob as a brother, I didn't want him to be my bodyguard. I didn't want Rick or Dan either, although Amelia had offered to hire bodyguards like them for me.

"I'm not going to art class or anywhere else. I'm grounded."

I wanted to be grounded. My only desire is to seclude myself in my room or get lost in the library surrounded by books.

I looked at Mom. She looked confused. "Okay, Adelina." She walked down the hallway and then up the steps and went into her office.

"I don't think so," Rob said. "This is not how it's going to go down."

"He's right, Adelina, you can't just hide. You need to live your life," Anne added.

"I'm calling the priest," Rob said.

"I'm going to my room," I said.

I went upstairs and sat on my bed. I pulled out my journal and wrote a pro and con list for staying home forever.

Pro

- I won't get kidnapped.
- I can read all the books in the library.
- I can sketch.

Cons

- I won't learn anything from the new art class.
- I might want to go outside sometimes.
- I won't ever see Irfan again.

Where did the last con come from? Why did that matter? I'm sure everyone was angry with me. I concealed information. Important information. It seems as if I have a talent for that. Yet, the grounding thing made little sense. Anne was right. I didn't view it as a form of punishment. What was punishment was the way I was feeling right now. Unsafe. Insecure.

There was a light knock on the door. "Adelina? It's Father Raphael. Can we talk?"

Here we go again, I thought. He's probably upset with me, too.

"Yeah, I'll be right out."

I stood up and opened the door. "Let's sit in the library," I said. I started down the stairs and stopped mid-step.

"What?" he said, bumping his knee into my back.

"Anne and Rob, oh, and Mom. I want them with us. I want them to know everything."

"Everything? Are you sure?"

"Yes, everything. Rob doesn't have a clue how dangerous the world of trafficking is, and Mom wants him to watch out for me."

"If you're sure."

We gathered in the library with steaming mugs of coffee and I told Rob and Anne *everything* mom already knew. Anne cried. A lot. Rob jumped up and paced around the table a few times. His face red, fists pumping the air. "They did what?" he said ten times.

"I need you to know, Rob. They can take you in the middle of the day. They can."

"Okay, I got it. I'm ready." He karate chopped the air. He still wasn't getting it. I jumped up, grabbed him around the throat, cut off his air supply, and watched him crumple to the ground.

Releasing my grip, he gasped for air.

"What the hell, Adelina?"

Mom didn't budge. Neither did Anne or Father. They observed with a mixture of shock and horror. I scanned their faces, unsure if they would shout or banish me to my room.

It was Father Raphael who finally spoke, "I think

what Adelina means by that is you need training if you are going out in the field with her."

"Sorry, Rob, you can't have my back if you don't know what you're doing."

"Okay, I get it. Did you have to almost kill me?"

"That was nothing," Father said. "You should see her with a knife." He winked at me.

"This is a dangerous thing we're doing, Rob. We have to be ready. Are you willing to train?" I said.

"Yes, I'm going to be a secret agent. Double o7." He snapped his fingers and stuck his hand out like a gun.

"Slow down, Rob. This isn't a game. It's not a video game," Mom said.

I remembered that feeling, like I was going to do something exciting and fun. I also remembered what came next. A whirlwind of planning, training, lying, betrayal, and ended with being kidnapped. I wonder if this is how Sabilia felt when she recruited me. Like, man this kid has no clue!

Now, Rob was dancing around the room, posing gangster style, I think.

Anne stood up. Her eyes were red and puffy. She leaned over and hugged me tightly. "I love you! I'm sorry you went through all of that. I'm here if you need to talk." With the last word trailing off, she sniffled, and bounded up the stairs, two at a time.

Mom sat with both hands wrapped around her mug. I wondered if she regretted adopting me. Bringing me into her secure, happy home.

Father broke into my reverie. "Okay, we train tomorrow. Call Irfan."

Rob stopped mid cycle. "Wait, what? You're going to train me?"

"He's not just a priest, you know that," I said.

"Irfan?" I said.

"He's already in the mix. Do you want him to get caught in a situation that he can't handle?" Mom said, finally contributing to the conversation.

"Yeah, you saw him. He's a wimp. A toothpick," Rob said.

"Don't say that," I said. Where did that come from and why did I care?

Rob and Father stepped onto the front porch to talk schedules.

Mom stood and wrapped her arm around my shoulder. "You did the right thing. You're a brave girl, Adelina. I wish this chapter of our lives were over. I'm sure you do too."

"Does that mean I'm ungrounded?"

She smiled a weak smile. "Yes, I guess that punishment is more of a blessing for you."

I laughed. "You can think up another punishment. Like dish duty or something."

"How about you come through this alive and your brother too?"

"I plan on it."

———

So, now, I stood frozen in my tracks in the doorway. The girl who choked her brother, afraid to go into a classroom.

He shoved me in. I lost my balance and caught

myself on a desk. With one smooth motion, I placed my backpack down and settled into a seat next to the professor's desk. Rob sat next to me.

We were wearing trackers. The guards stationed outside were dressed in hoodies and jeans, trying their best to blend in. Dad's idea. He insisted. "We're not losing our girl again," he had said.

Everyone else looked nervous, too. It made me feel better. They were nervous about the first day of class, the girls fixing their hair, checking their phones. The guys seemed too nonchalant, as if they deliberately calculated their actions. I was wearing a new outfit that Cecylia had picked out for me. Skinny jeans, sandals and a green sleeveless top. "You don't want to look like you're trying too hard," she said, whatever that meant. Trying too hard to look like a college student or trying too hard to break up a human trafficking ring?

A girl wearing a hijab motioned to my backpack which was taking up a seat. The room was filling up quickly. I grabbed it and she slid into the seat and smiled at me. "I'm Natasha."

"Hi," I smiled back. "I'm Adelina."

"Foreign exchange student too, huh?" she said.

"Uhh, no, I'm not."

"Oh, the accent. I thought…" Her voice trailed off. "Nevermind. Glad to meet you. I think we shall be good friends. You like art, huh?"

"Yes, I do. This is my brother, Robert."

He leaned over and said, "You can call me Rob. Everyone else does."

"Hello, class, welcome to art 101. I'm Tracey, your instructor. Before I go through the roll. We have a few changes. Professor Cohen has gone over your portfolios and it looks like a few of you will advance to 102 today." Her wavy auburn hair concealed her face while she looked down and shuffled some papers.

"Here we go," she pulled up a single sheet of paper. Her eyes were like blue ice. She wore a faded jean jacket over a graphic tee, skinny jeans, and ankle boots. She looked more like a student than a teacher.

"Alright, if I call your name, please come to the front of the class. Natasha Bahri."

Natasha stood and grinned.

"Adelina Hunter."

I stood. My face flushed. Really? I was moving up?

Rob stood. "I'm coming too."

"Looks like that's it. Girls come with me." Natasha and I made our way to the front of the class.

"I'll deliver these students toProfessor Cohen and be back with you in a minute. Please stay seated." she added .

Rob bounded up to the front of the class. "I don't think I called your name, young man. There were just two girls' names." The class tittered.

"This is my sister." He put his hand on my shoulder. "I'm going with her."

"Son, this is college. I think your sister is all grown up. She can handle it." The class laughed again. Rob's cool exterior vanished and his shoulders slumped in defeat.

Natasha leaned towards him and whispered, "I'll sit by her and keep an eye on her."

Rob walked back to his seat and pulled out his

phone. I glanced at him one last time, but he didn't look up. He was most likely texting the team.

Natasha, Tracey, and I walked down the hallway. "Right in here." she said. We were only two doors down from Rob. It didn't look like he needed to worry.

"Smile," Natasha said. "This is a great honor!" I smiled and relaxed a little. She was right. I wasn't walking into a sex trafficking ring. Just an art class without my brother. My newly trained, freshly, recruited brother.

Tracey left us at the door. "Go in and find a seat. The professor is expecting you."

Natasha and I found seats in the back. I saw a familiar dark head in the second row. He turned. It was Irfan. He waved and smiled and patted an empty seat next to him.

I shook my head. He hung his head in mock shame and then smiled. "See you after class." he mouthed.

Natasha stuck her elbow in my rib. "You move fast, quiet girl."

"What? No. That's my brother's friend."

The whiteboard at the front of the room caught my attention. The professor had his back towards us. He was writing. I reached in my bag and pulled out my notebook and a pen.

He was blond. Well built. He wore faded jeans, boots, and a blazer. He looked more like a professor than Tracey. At least the back of him. As soon as he turned around to speak to the class, my heart sank. I felt sick.

Ryszard. What? How? I felt dizzy.

"The greatest evils in the world will not be carried

out by people with guns, but by men in suits sitting behind desks."

Why did this quote come to me now? Suddenly, I was back in the orphanage library sitting with Professor Wroblewski, a retired literature professor from Warsaw University. He shared with me his experience facing enemy Nazis during World War II. "You face your enemy with a smile on your face, a pure heart, and a plan in your mind to defeat them long term."

Winston Churchill had said, "You have enemies? Good. That means you've stood up for something, sometime in your life." My enemy was right here in front of me. I tried to remember everything the professor had ever told me about facing the enemy. This was going to be tough.

"Hey," Natasha said, her voice sounded far away like she was in a tunnel. "Are you okay?"

I felt myself slipping in my seat. Falling. Natasha pulled me back up. I took a deep breath. I grabbed my water bottle and chugged some.

I admitted, "I shouldn't have skipped breakfast," and attempted to stifle a laugh.

"Yeah."

She focused on Ryszard. He was lecturing. Natasha took notes. Irfan typed notes on a laptop. I didn't know what else to do, so I wrote notes as well. Could my life be any more messed up?

A guy to the left of me raised his hand and answered that Sir Isaac Newton painted the Mona Lisa. How did that kid get into the advanced class? I don't have the mental capacity to think about that right now. How did this all come about? How did a wanted sex trafficker from Poland manage to become an art professor, and why would he do so openly? Was he aware that I had registered for the class? Obviously, he knew I was here. He had kept his back turned while the T.A. called roll. He had heard my name. Why here? Was he trying to hide away? Or had he infiltrated the university as a ruse to find me? Maybe he had a new computer genius who could doctor papers and that sort of stuff. My poetry brain was in overdrive.

"Miss Hunter, what is your opinion on this piece?"

My head jerked up from my notes. "I, Um…."

"Painting is poetry that is seen rather than felt, and poetry is painting that is felt rather than seen."[2]

Nice of you to quote the artist about his own work. A wave of laughter swept across the room. I put my head down.

"Do you think you could tell us about the art, Miss Hunter?"

"It's the study for the head of Christ for the Last Supper."

"Good job, Miss Hunter."

He clicked to the next frame.

How was I going to survive this class twice a week? What was our strategy for taking down an art professor who was engaged in human trafficking? Irfan turned and gave me a thumbs up.

"Mr. Pasha, maybe you'd like to handle the next one?"

Irfan swiveled forward a little too quickly in his seat and caught himself before he tipped over.

"Well, I….Saint John the Baptist," he sighed.

"Great." And Ryszard went on teaching. Wait. What was his name? I pulled out the syllabus that had been left on the desk. Professor Cohen, that's right. That's what Tracey had said.

I couldn't wait to get out of class. Nothing was going to prevent me from keeping this information to myself. Nothing.

"We have a study group at my place Wednesday. You'll get an email about the specifics. I expect all of you to be there. Especially those who think Sir Isaac Newton painted the Mona Lisa."

"He's cute and funny," Natasha whispered. I grabbed my backpack and said nothing.

Ryszard, Professor Cohen, or whoever he was, was the first to exit the room. I took my time. Natasha rushed off to another class and said she would see me at the study group the next day. Irfan waved and motioned to his phone as he ran out the door. He must have a class too. I breathed a sigh of relief. I wanted to find Rob and go home.

The hallway was quiet. I walked toward a blinking exit sign and pushed the door. Someone came up behind me, grabbed my shirt, and pushed me into a darkened corner.

"I'm back," Ryszard said and grinned his evil grin. "You thought you killed me. You thought you took me down?"

I pushed back. "Get your hands off me."

"Why? Because you have little FBI guards in my class who don't know one thing about art?" That answered the question about the guy in the plaid shirt.

"Why here Ryszard? Why?"I was acting tough. Inside I was jello. Hot jello that didn't set. I could feel it swish around in my gut and sneak up my throat.

"I couldn't let you go, knowing what you know. I have some sweet opportunities here. And, if you tell your lovely little family - I will kill every one of them. And the priest. And who is that they are looking for? Aneta, ah yes, I'll kill her too in a particularly fun way."

I gasped for breath and tried to back away. I heard the clack of heels coming down the hall. Ryszard backed off and pasted on a smile.

"Adelina, hey!"

"Natasha, I thought you went to class." I wanted to jump up and down and shout, "Thank you for coming back!" Instead, I took a deep breath and tried to be calm, cool, and collected.

"I left my phone in class," she explained

Ryszard opened the door, stepped out, and he was gone.

CHAPTER
FIVE

THE RESURGENCE

I stepped out the double glass doors of the Creative Arts Center with Natasha. I scanned the sidewalk and parking lot for Ryszard. Nothing. He was gone.

"Do you know Rysz… I mean Professor Cohen?"

"Nope. First class with him. I think this is his first semester here. He is pretty cute, huh? I think he's from Poland."

"Hmmm," I said, scanning the sidewalk for Rob now.

"Hey, aren't you Polish? I mean, the accent."

"Oh, yeah. I am. I was adopted."

"Cool."

"Where are you from?"

"Pakistan."

"That's awesome," I said it with my mouth but my brain was somewhere else.

Distracted- unable to concentrate because one's mind is preoccupied.

I needed Rob or Anne.

I could feel a poem coming on. I didn't want Natasha to think I was a weirdo, but there was no stopping it. I need Father Raphael. I didn't know what to do. These days, I seem to be constantly turning to him, or maybe God, I'm not sure. Did I grab the obvious FBI guy who was loitering near the glass double doors? He acted like he was scoping out girls. He was way too obvious, or I was getting better at noticing details. Did I try calling Sabilia and tell her everything? I wasn't hiding any information this time. She could get my family to a safe house. Or did I play along with Ryszard's wishes to take down the whole human trafficking ring?

"What?" Natasha said loudly, wrecking my train of thought.

You said, "There is a twofold Silence- sea and shore- Body and soul".

"Oh, I did? ... Yeah, that's for another class. Sorry."

"Poe, right?"

"Yes, it's Poe."

There are some qualities- some incorporate things,
That have a double life, which thus is made
A type of that twin entity which springs
From matter and light, evinced in solid and shade.
There is a twofold Silence- sea and shore-
Body and soul. One dwells in lonely places,
Newly with grass o'ergrown; some solemn graces,
Some human memories and tearful lore,
Render him terrorless: his name's "No More."
He is the corporate Silence: dread him not!
No power hath he of evil in himself;

But should some urgent fate (untimely lot!)
Bring thee to meet his shadow (nameless elf,
That haunteth the lone regions where hath trod
No foot of man,) commend thyself to God![1]

She recited the first half, and I joined in. It was oddly comforting to recite out loud. It helped me think. I wouldn't face the terror alone and I wouldn't stay silent. I wasn't falling into that trap.

Rob finally came out of the building, sandwiched between two girls. They were giggling, and he was walking like a pufferfish, his chest all stuck out. What was he doing?

"Hey, Adelina!" He made his way over to me with the girls in tow. They didn't stop giggling. What did Rob say that was so funny?

"Hey, this is Misty and this is Krissy."

"This is Natasha." I grabbed his sleeve and dragged him away from his new parasites. Their giggles only subsided when he was ten feet away. Geez.

"I have to tell you something. It's super important. First, see the plaid shirt guy over by the door?"

"Yes," he said, jerking his head in that direction.

"Don't be so obvious!" I pulled him further away. "He is FBI. Do you know why there would be an FBI guy in my art class?"

Right as I was about to tell him, a brief rush of air passed by my head, like a buzzing fly. The FBI guy went down. He grabbed his arm and a crimson splotch grew, eating up the blue plaid.

"He's been shot!" Natasha yelled. "This guy has been shot."

The giggling girls ran screaming.

My phone rang. I answered. "Adelina, you aren't telling, are you? This minor flesh wound is just a teaser. Tell and people die. Important people. People close to you." Blood drained from my face. I felt sick all over again. When would I escape this madness? It followed me here. I didn't have to worry about my reaction now. Everyone was busy with their own things.

I ran over to the plaid FBI guy and kneeled down next to him.

"It's just a flesh wound," he said through gritted teeth.

"I called 911!" Rob said, holding up his phone as proof.

"Was this a terrorist attack?" Someone yelled and pointed at Irfan, who was running toward us.

"Is everyone okay?" Irfan yelled.

"It was Ryszard," I whispered into plaid shirt's ear. His facial expression changed from pain to shock.

An ambulance screamed up the parking lot.

"You need to come with me," the FBI guy said, grabbing my arm.

"No, you need to stay away from me," I said. I stood up and walked back to Rob. "Let's get out of here."

"Our first day on campus, there's a shooting!" Natasha said.

"Irfan, come on." I yelled.

I ran down the sloped parking lot and pushed the button to cross the four lanes to the Coliseum. Rob, Irfan, and Natasha followed me.

"Why are we running?" Rob asked. "Shouldn't we stay and help?"

"I don't know about you, but I'm running cause I'm Middle Eastern and someone just got shot."

"Me too," said Natasha.

Good, they had other reasons. I didn't have to worry about explaining everything to them en route. If it wasn't such a dangerous situation, I would have laughed.

Laugh-make the spontaneous sounds and movements of the face and body that are the instinctive expressions of lively amusement and sometimes also of contempt or derision.

Rob paused. "Wait. Where are we going?"

I hadn't thought that out. I was just running.

"Anne isn't picking us up for another hour."

"Oh." I whispered, putting both my hands on my knees and breathing hard. I guess we look kind of suspicious. Running from a shooting. This is one of many reasons I needed Rob. He could think well under pressure instead of just reciting definitions and poems.

We stood in the middle of the Coliseum parking lot as an ambulance whizzed by. We all just looked at each other for a minute. A campus cop strode toward us.

"Hey, you!" He pointed at us. "I need your statements. Did you see what happened? Where did the bullet come from? Why are you running?"

"Sorry, sir, we were just not sure if the shooting part was over," Rob said.

"Understandable. How about we go inside and sit down?"

My knees buckled, and I hit the ground.

I woke up on something hard. Was it a cot? I jerked

my arms. No chains. Was I having a flashback? I rolled off of the wood and hit the floor.

"Hey, Adelina, it's okay. You're okay. I'm here."

Rob picked me up and set me on the bench and wrapped a blanket around me. "You passed out."

"She didn't eat breakfast," Natasha said.

"Oh, with the stress of the incident, that makes sense," the cop said. "Get this girl a snack and a drink."

Irfan left and came back a few minutes later with a coffee and a granola bar.

"I've called a nurse to check you out," the campus cop said. "Drink your coffee. Do you think you would be up to answering a few questions?"

"I didn't see anything." I said. "He crumpled to the ground. The guy in the plaid shirt. That's it."

"Can we go now?" Rob asked. "She knows nothing. It just upset her. This is her first day here."

"Yes, you can all go. I have all your info in case I need to contact you. Oh, here's the nurse."

He turned to let a brunette lady in scrubs pass.

"Let's check you out," she said.

She took out a blood pressure cuff and stethoscope.

A half an hour later, we were in Anne's car heading home. I couldn't wait to get home. The nurse had said I was fine and reminded me to always eat breakfast. I was quiet on the way home. What could I say?

"By the way, Professor Cohen is Ryszard. He's going to kill all of us, but it will happen a lot quicker if I tell you who he is."

Natasha had given me her number and gone home, too. Irfan tagged along with us, "to make sure I was okay," he said. Whatever that meant.

Mom met us at the back door. Anne had texted her that there was a shooting on campus and that we were okay.

"Were you the target?" was the first thing Mom said.

"No, Mom. NO. It had nothing to do with me." I lied.

Here we go again, I thought. The lying. I couldn't do this. I was going to find out a way to tell Mom, Dad, Sabilia, and Father the truth. How long could Ryszard keep up the charade, anyway? People on the task force knew what he looked like. Obviously, the FBI was onto him. He shot an FBI agent. That wasn't going away.

"Sorry, Mom, I'm just tired. Can we talk about this later?"

I started up the stairs to my room.

"Oh, no dearie, you come back down here."

"MOMMMMM!"

"Yes, we can talk about it later, but you need to eat. You passed out today."

"I could eat," I said, calming down. The trauma pediatrician mom had taken me to said that I didn't recognize my body's own signals. I didn't recognize thirst and hunger. Weird. Yet another odd thing about me. Mom had said she was going to set a timer on my phone to remind me to eat and drink every two hours. I had talked her out of it, but I didn't think that was going to stick anymore.

I ate a turkey and spinach wrap, drank a cup of Mom's strong coffee, and avoided looking her in the eye. I took the napkin she gave me and sketched on it while we talked at the island. She sat beside me on a stool, which helped with my inability to make eye contact. Rather than maintaining direct eye contact, I could occasionally glance sideways in a socially acceptable manner.

"So, I hear you got bumped up a class?"

"Yep, along with a new girl I met, Natasha."

"Oh, a new friend. You'll have to have her over."

"Really? Yeah, I will. That would be cool. So, I'll see her at the study group tomorrow at Professor Cohen's house." My face got all hot and red when I said Professor Cohen. I'd almost forgotten about attending the study group. The unexpected reminder about Ryszard's house took me by surprise and plunged me into a spiral of fear. If mom noticed, she didn't say anything.

Rob and Irfan had been outside. They came in the back door and Rob said, "Hey, Adelina, we set up the hammocks in the back. Come take a rest!"

"Sure," That sounds good. "Thanks, Mom. Talk later?"

"Yes, go on and I'll be adding the reminder to your phone. Eat and drink every two hours."

I walked out the back door and down the hill to the trio of hammocks hung in a triangle. I slipped my shoes off and slid in, and pulled the extra material over my face. I didn't want to talk to anyone. I needed to process.

"Hey, did you bring your phone down?" Rob asked.

"Uh, yeah, I think so."

"Hand it over. You too Irfan." We both handed our phones over. Rob turned and sprinted up to the house with them.

Five minutes later, he made his way back to us with a jug of apple cider and some plastic cups.

"Just in case," he said matter-of-factly.

"In case what?" Irfan asked.

"Someone is listening or tracking us or something. I saw it in a movie."

"Oh," Irfan said, and then leaned back in the hammock.

"So, are we going to talk about what happened to us today or what?"

"Nope." I said.

"Okay." Rob said and leaned back. "But wait till Dad gets home and we *will* be talking about it. We'd better all have the same story."

"There is no story."

I woke to the leaves crunching. I peered out of my cocoon. Someone was coming down the hill.

I sat up. Irfan and Rob did the same.

"Irfan?"

"Yes," he mumbled.

Two broad shouldered FBI jacket clad men towered over us. "You need to come with us. You're wanted for questioning."

"What?" he squeaked.

"You were involved in the terrorist attack on the RMU campus earlier today."

He said it like a statement. Like a fact. My mind raced. I went back over the scenario. Irfan ran toward us from the parking lot after the shot. Did he do it? Could we trust him?

Irfan fell out of the hammock and righted himself. "I should have listened to my father," he whispered.

"HOLD on," a deep voice bellowed from the top of the hill. It was Dad. He marched down the hill. "What's going on here? Where are you taking this boy?"

"We believe *this boy* was involved in a terrorist attack on the campus today. He shot an FBI agent."

"What?!" Dad looked stunned. I guess Mom hadn't filled him in yet about the shooting. I hadn't filled her in about the FBI agent thing.

And I didn't think anyone would mention the FBI agent attending my art class, anyway. He was undercover.

I said nothing. I was too busy racing through second thoughts and third thoughts. The cars in the parking lot. Irfan ran towards us. The look of terror on his face.

"Why would he shoot a man and then run towards him?"

"What?"

Everyone looked at me. "Yeah, he came to see if the guy was okay."

"Right, I did," Irfan said in his own defense.

The agents had Irfan by the elbows. They froze. Everyone froze. I guess I gave them something to think about.

"We still have to take him in." They dragged him up the hill. Irfan let his knees scrape the ground and gather leaves like a rake.

Dad followed. "I'm calling someone about this. Irfan, give me your parents' info, please." Irfan spouted off some numbers and dad punched them into his phone.

By now, Rob and I were running up the hill. FBI

guys stuffed Irfan in the back of a dark SUV and took off down the road, leaving a trail of dust.

THE RALLY

Rob and I stuffed the hammocks back in their pouches and hiked up the hill. Dad met us halfway up.

"We need to talk," Dad said.

"Yeah, I guess we do," Rob said.

I kept going up the hill and walked right past the both of them. I could feel Dad's eyes boring through my back. My face and neck, hot from the exertion and the lying. I knew he knew. How could parents do that? I hadn't even been part of the family for an entire year yet and Dad could read me like a dictionary. I laughed out loud.

"What's so funny?" a voice said from the top of the hill. All I could see was pink. Pink jeans and pink ankle boots.

"Cecylia!" I ran up to her and grabbed her in a hug. "I made a mom joke, that's all." I don't know why I hugged her. I stepped back, embarrassed. I guess I felt like she knew. She understood what it was like to live two lives. To live a lie. It was all about to "hit the fan," as Rob would say. I wasn't sure what that meant. I needed to get a new dictionary for all this slang.

"So, there was a shooting and you are making jokes and hugging me?" Cecylia said and put her hands on her hips. "Is this just normal stuff for us now?"

"No. I guess I'm glad to see someone who under-stands violence and chaos."

"Thanks. I think. Not sure if that is a compliment."

Frick and Frack joined us and we all went into the house together.

"We're going to meet Sabilia," Mom said as we came in. "She says we need to meet somewhere else. I guess she'll explain when we get there. She said to dress warmly."

Mom filled a thermos with coffee and packed a basket full of sandwiches.

"What about Irfan?" I asked.

"Don't worry. We'll address that when we get there," Mom said and put a finger to her lips to shush me.

"Well, that outfit looks super cute on you!" Cecylia added.

I was learning Cecylia's ways. When she needed to not talk about the "elephant in the room" (mom's phrase), she got shallow and talked about clothes and makeup.

So, someone bugged our house then. Our phones too. But, I knew about the phone thing. At least that's what social media said. The FBI listened to everything, now I wasn't sure if they were on our side or not. I didn't know who was on what side. I'm glad I had a family, including Cecylia, Sabilia, Father, and Kasia. They were my support team, no, something more than that. I didn't know what to call them, so I stuck with "team."

"Yes," I said. "Thanks for picking this out for me when we went shopping. I am going to change, though. Dress warmly?"

I went upstairs and shut the door to my room. It suddenly felt unsafe. Like the walls were listening. The first person I thought of was Professor Wrobleski. I opened my journal and flipped through some pages. I had copied a quote by C.S. Lewis that the professor had used to explain life in the ghetto in Warsaw.

"Mental pain is less dramatic than physical pain, but it is more common and also more hard to bear."

He had said that the mental strain of the war was worse than the fear of getting shot. Most people didn't know who they could trust, including him. Who was working for the Nazis? Who wasn't? Hadn't I just doubted Irfan? Which side was he on? I pulled some gray leggings on and grabbed a lime green wool sweater. What was I going to tell everyone at the meeting? Where was this mysterious meeting going to take place? Did I tell everyone the truth and risk everyone getting shot? Or did I make truth my plumb-line and let the task force work out a plan?

I didn't know. I grabbed my journal and slid it back into its hiding place behind the head of the sleigh bed. Anne had made me a secret cloth pocket that was velcroed behind the top of the curve of the bed. I loved it. It made me feel safer to write my thoughts. I put my phone there too, just for now. Rob's statement about the phones and Cecylia's diva mode had me freaked out.

Back downstairs, Mom and Dad were putting hiking boots on. "Where are we going?" I said, and I instantly regretted it when I saw their faces.

Cecylia saved the moment. "Just out in the yard. You guys need to rake. It's looking awful. Come on, tell me all about your first day of school."

She held up a piece of paper. It said -

Leave your phone here.

The alarm on my watch buzzed loudly, scaring the pee out of me. "Oh, I need to eat and drink something," I said. Mom reached over and took my watch off, handed me a pack of crackers, and a water bottle.

Oh yeah, my watch had a GPS in it. Wow, this was getting super creepy. I liked it better when I had no technology.

We went out the front door. Dad locked it and armed the system. I wasn't sure what good that would do against Ryszard. I'm sure he found another computer whiz here in the states to replace Cecylia. At least we had her on our team.

We loaded into the Suburban, "kits, cats, sacks, and wives," as Mom said. I thought the conversation would start once we got on our way, but it didn't. Mom turned on Vivaldi's *Four Seasons* and no one spoke. The music transported me back to the children's home, the library where I had listened to bits of the *Four Seasons* on an old cassette tape that had bits of rap recorded over it. I enjoyed listening to the whole selection. It was calming.

Mom shared my love of classical music. She listened to it on Amazon Prime while she wrote. She had also introduced me to some opera through *Opera for People who Hate Opera*. I loved it. Sometimes, we cleaned the house to those CDs and sang parts of it at the top of our lungs, off key. Rob wouldn't want his friends to know, but he sometimes joined us, dancing around the kitchen to the *Overture of William Tell* as if he were riding a horse. Anne had no qualms about it belting out tunes, no matter where we were or who was there. Lucy and Ivan, my niece and nephew, loved opera. They asked for it often when they visited. Family. An amazing thing. We shared music. Laughter. Meals. Holidays. I just wish my past had stayed in Poland where it belonged instead of following me here. My family had to share that too.

Forty minutes later, we pulled into Red Squirrel Rock State Forest. We unloaded the SUV and each carried something. Baskets of food. A carafe of coffee. Backpacks and sweatshirts. Everyone remained eerily silent.

We followed the trail to Red Squirrel City, a cropping of enormous boulders that attract repellers and amateur climbers like Rob and some of his buddies. It was a short hike. Rob and Dad lead the way. Mom, Cecylia, and me, behind them. Mom linked arms with us girls when she could. When the path narrowed and we had to walk through boulders, I took the lead. Of course, Frick and Frack were everywhere at once, hopping from rock to rock. Thankfully, they wore hikers' gear instead of suits. To the naked eye, we looked like a family and friends on an outing instead of a task force on a mission. I guess that was the point.

Mom, Cecylia, and I laid some wool plaid blankets on large flat rocks. Mom passed tiny cups of coffee around. I passed out carrot cake muffins while we waited for Sabilia and Father Raphael.

I sipped my coffee and held on to the cup for warmth. The temperature contrast between our house and the state park was insane. It was fifteen degrees colder here. I should be anxious. I should freak out, but here I was sipping coffee and talking about my art class. The shooting of the FBI agent felt like a lifetime ago. It felt like a different universe when they took Irfan in for questioning. I sure knew how to pick friends.

Three guys squeezed out of the crevice between two giant rocks. It was the two FBI agents who had taken Irfan from our woods. Irfan was between them. They were laughing, chatting. Chatting. Why were they chatting? Hadn't they taken him in for questioning forceably? I mean, hadn't he resisted and all of that? The agents had changed into L.L. Bean khakis and boots. Both of them wore red L.L. Bean jackets. "Way to stick out like twins," Irfan said.

One of the *twins* punched him on the arm, sending Irfan knocking into the other twin. "Watch it pipsqueak!" the other *twin* replied. Irfan also wore L.L. Bean gear. My mind tried to make sense of this picture.

"Hey, guys!" Irfan said. "Good news. I'm not under arrest."

Sabilia and Father Raphael stepped out of the rock enclosure.

"I see you all have met the rest of the team," Sabilia said. I hated when she did that. She talked as if everyone always knew what was going on. I didn't know what was going on. What was going on!?

"Hey, what the hell is going on?" Rob said, as if he had read my mind. He had pulled himself up to his full height. He looked like dad. Broad shouldered and full of authority.

"Simmer down, son," Dad said. "We will explain in a minute. No, Sabilia, we don't know the rest of the team. We haven't filled the kids in."

"Wait. What?" I said. Cecylia stood, too. "You adults know what is going on and we don't?"

"If everyone will stop talking, we can explain," Sabilia said.

"MOM? DAD?" I wasn't ready to let it go.

"Listen, honey," Mom said. She stood and patted me on the back. "We were going to fill you in as soon as we got somewhere we could talk. We couldn't talk at home."

"Right now, there's a crew going over our house looking for bugs," Dad added.

"Irfan?" Rob said and waited for an explanation. Our suspicions were accurate. Our home was bugged.

"Okay, you deserve an explanation. Could I have some coffee, Mrs. Hunter? I'm freezing. Then I will tell all."

Mom handed him a cup of coffee and we all took a seat.

"I'm not a foreign exchange student. I'm an FBI agent."

"What?" I said, "You lied?" *said the liar.*

"Not about everything," he said, looking gooey-eyed in my direction. The twin agents snickered.

Irfan turned bright red and then continued. "I am on a task force. Our focus is human trafficking as it applies to terrorist groups." As he talked, he transformed from a skinny, awkward teen to an astute, knowledgeable agent.

astute-having or showing an ability to accurately assess situations or people and turn this to one's advantage.

Once again, my mind retraced our interactions from the beginning. The bonfire. The texts. The pieces of the puzzle were there. I wasn't sure how they fit.

"But," interrupted Rob, "you're a teenager."

"Yes, I am, and so are you. You and Adelina are on a task force."

"Oh, yeah. Wait. We went through training together."

"Yes, I kind of faked my ineptitude."

"Oh." Rob was quiet after that.

"Can we get to the point of this meeting?" Sabilia said. "The sun is about to set."

"Right," said Irfan. "I am posing as a student. We found out Ryszard was coming to this area. He is on campus."

Man, it was so good to hear those words.

"So, you know he is posing as a professor?" I said.

"Yes," Irfan said. "We do and we also know he is working with a larger organization. We want to take them down. The tricky part was protecting you at the same time."

"Yes, we did not know that you would be placed in

his class," Thing One said. I was hoping at some point the twins would introduce themselves. Until they did, I called them Thing One and Thing Two, as in the Dr. Suess book.

"Father Raphael had tasked us with finding Aneta. We did. But, she seems to be embedded in the organization. She is either great at pretending or she is working for Ryszard in his new venture."

"What is his new venture?" Dad asked.

"Selling college students to terrorist groups. Mostly. Sometimes there isn't a sale, just lots of threats to the effect of 'we will kill your family if you don't ______" Sabilia said. "We think that is the hold he has on Aneta."

"We hope," Father Raphael said.

"So, the FBI and the Internal Task Force have joined forces to take down Ryszard and a few terrorists to boot," Dad said.

"Exactly, and I am the scapegoat, so Ryszard doesn't know we're on to him. He just thinks I'm a foreign exchange student. A Muslim as well. I am neither." He laughed.

"Dad, who did you call if it wasn't Irfan's father?" asked Rob.

"It was an encrypted number. Our tech guys made it look like he was calling Saudi Arabia and Irfan's father 'answered'." Thing One said.

"Yep and he is on his way to the states right now."

"From?" Rob said.

"Pittsburgh, PA," Irfan smiled. "Yep, I was born and raised there. Dad is going to drive here from the airport and bail me out."

It turns out the FBI booked a flight for Irfan's dad, who was replaced by a double in Saudi Arabia, and would take the flight. Irfan's father would change places with him and drive to campus. Actually, Nathaniel's father, Nathaniel, is his real name which we weren't to use.

They recruited Irfan at his private school in Pittsburgh because of his amazing aptitude to remember everything, faces, dates, etc. He had a photographic memory, and he looked Middle Eastern. That was a plus. He flew through training and at seventeen he was on his first assignment, here in West Virginia.

The sun slipped behind the rock formations and the temperature dropped another ten degrees.

"We need to wrap this up," Sabilia said.

"What's next?" Cecylia asked. She had been surprisingly quiet during the meeting. It wasn't like her not to "put in her two cents," a phrase I picked up from Anne.

"Next is, Adelina, you go to class and study group and find out what you can find out," Sabilia said. "Cecylia, we need you to be on call on campus to help Adelina and Rob whenever they need you. We can't have the place crawling with agents. Ryszard will get suspicious."

"Irfan, looks like you get locked up until Daddy gets here," Thing One said, elbowing him in the ribs.

"Right, we need to make this look real," Sabilia explained.

"Nothing is real," Cecylia said. "We came to the states to get away from this and it just followed us here." She started sobbing.

"Wait," I said, "Cecylia, you are the reason I'm alive.

You don't want other girls to go through what we went through, do you?"

"Of .... course ... .not," she sobbed. "I'm just not as strong as you, Adelina. I'm not."

Me? Adelina. Who was she talking about? Another Adelina?

I looked at Father Raphael and nodded my head toward Cecylia. He was the priest, why wasn't he doing his priest thing? Had this whole Aneta thing swallowed him up?

"I don't want to do this. It's your turn to do it. It's something you're really skilled at. You don't need me." she added.

"We need you Cecylia!" I said. "If nothing else, I need you to be my friend. You're more than a friend. You're a kindred spirit."

Father Raphael still hadn't moved.

"Hey, aren't you that computer genius?" Thing One asked.

"Yes, yes she is," Mom said.

"Yep," I added.

"Oh man, we need you. Word is you know all about Ryszard's dealings on the Darknet. Can you help us?"

Cecylia looked up and wiped her eyes. "I suppose I could help in that way. I just never want to have to see that man again."

I understood. I didn't either. I didn't blame Cecylia for wanting to quit. I wanted to quit. I remembered the upcoming study group, and I felt a wave of terror wash over me. I grabbed a muffin and stuffed it in my mouth. I swallowed a sizable chunk, hoping it would push the fear down with it.

"Great. We have a computer lab right off campus. If you could come help us out, please," he smiled.

"Well, since you asked so nicely," she said, and she was back to her perky, normal self.

We hiked back to the parking lot as the shadowy darkness descended on the boulders. Thing One and Thing Two shoved Irfan back into their SUV. They were enjoying pushing him around. He seemed to be a good sport, though.

Cecylia and I linked arms. "You know what we need?" I asked.

"What?"

"We need another shopping day and a movie night." I said. I sometimes forget that Cecylia had lived a normal life until last year. Her life experience had been a close knit family, family meals, shopping, and very little stress. My life has been one stressful thing after another. I was used to living in survival mode. She wasn't.

"I agree," Mom said. "We need some girl time!" She took my elbow. We looked like family and friends on a fun outing, despite the FBI agents, the task force, the bodyguards, and the fake terrorist. Oh, and a priest with a gun. What a weird tribe.

CHAPTER
SEVEN

THE REVELATION

It was our first study group at Professor Cohen's. I had to repeat his name to myself often or I would call him Ryszard or worse, Scary Guy. Natasha stood by me as I knocked on the door of the old craftsman in South Park. A fellow student answered the door.

"There's no reason to knock," she said with a smile. "Come in, coffee is over here," she pointed to a shaker style table with coffee, cream, sugar and an assortment of cookies. "Help yourself, then come join us in the den." And she was gone.

Natasha giggled. "Look at this house," she said. "Everything is so gorgeous. The floors must be original." She pointed to the hardwood.

The house was impressive. Rys.. I mean, Professor Cohen had done his homework. This is just the type of house I imagined a professor owning. Original woodwork. Bookcases -full of books. Art decorated every wall. Copies, but art. Weird. *Be normal.* I told myself.

Natasha was animatedly talking about books and art. With a cup of coffee in hand, I braced myself to enter the den and confront Professor Cohen.

Prepare-make (something) ready for use or consideration.

"Are you ready?" I said. Natasha grabbed her coffee and grinned.

"Yep."

We walked through the pocket doors. Some students sat on leather couches while others lounged on over-sized pillows on the floor. A girl immediately caught my attention. She occupied the seat beside Ryszard who sat in an espresso brown leather chair, just like the one Mom had in the library. She called it mid-century modern. Funny, I wasn't as shaky seeing him as I expected to be. Maybe my level of Ryszard tolerance was different in a room full of peers. He was talking about Da Vinci. The girl. Back to the girl. Aneta. It had to be her. Her hair was longer than the photo I had seen. It was a different color, too. Brunette instead of blonde like Sabilia's. She looked more grown up than the picture too, which made sense. She wasn't fifteen anymore. She had to be seventeen or eighteen. I tried to get a read on her. There was no sign of fear in her expression. She looked like a student. Ripped skinny jeans and a long sweater with bell sleeves. She wore no shoes, just orange and brown patterned wool socks.

"What's going on in there?" I jerked around and looked at Natasha, who was making googly eyes at Professor Cohen. Great. She's fallen under his spell. How was I going to handle this? It suddenly hit me - the earbud! Cecylia was on the receiving end.

"Can't talk right now," I said with gritted teeth.

"I know, right," Natasha answered me. "It's so over-whelming. Like in a good way, right?"

That's not how I would describe it. Like a lamb led to the slaughter was more like it.

"Yeah, right. Let's find a spot where we can hear more clearly," I said, more for the sake of Cecylia than Natasha.

Up to this point, we had been standing awkwardly at the open pocket doors.

Aneta waved and motioned to some floor space near her. I didn't know if she knew who I was or if she was just being friendly. How does a mind make sense of these sorts of things, period?

"Once I wished I might rehearse
Freedom's paean in my verse,
That the slave who caught the strain
Should throb until he snapped his chain.
But the Spirit said, 'Not so;[1]

"What did you say, Adelina?" Professor Cohen and Cecylia asked in stereo.

I looked up. "What?"

"You're doing that poetry thing again," Cecylia said.

"You said, but the spirit said, not so," Rszyard said. "Was that in reference to Da Vinci or something else?"

"Da Vinci," I said, "the deeper the feeling, the greater the pain." I said. All eyes turned toward me. All the blood rose from my feet and settled in a hot red kiln comprising my neck and face. I was pretty sure, along with the beading sweat on my forehead, that steam escaped with each word.

"So right, you quote the master himself. The more

we feel the art, the more emotions we can experience, even if it happens to be pain. What did you mean about the spirit?" Professor Cohen said.

"Oh, that was Ralph Waldo Emerson. I mean sometimes we want to experience freedom from the slavery of our circumstance." I replied, cradling my mug. I squeezed it so hard I thought it would crack or I would.

"What are you doing?" Cecylia said in my ear. "Stop goading him."

"Or slavery in general," I added.

What was I doing?

"Right. The slavery of ignorance. Of not being able to enjoy art." Natasha said. She was shaking in agreement like a bobble head.

Could no one else but Cecylia and I feel the tension? Ryszard smiled at me as if I were just a student contributing a brilliant point. I glanced at Aneta. Was that a micro-expression of pain?

The study group droned on with no more incidents. When Professor Cohen wrapped it up, several students made their way over to Natasha and me. They introduced themselves. I lost track of names after the first three.

"Ashley," one auburn-haired girl said. "Great point. Cool that you know poetry. I love it!"

"Courtney," said a raven-haired, chocolate-skinned girl. "Nice to meet you. I think we have 102 together."

I discovered that the study group was for multiple classes taught by Professor Cohen. So, the people I was meeting, I was likely only to see at the study group.

"Are you keeping track of everyone?" Cecylia said.

"I'm trying," I whispered.

"Does anyone look enslaved?"

"What do you mean, enslaved?" I said a little too loudly.

"Right, enslaved, awesome point, I'm Lauren."

"Stop talking to me, Cecylia. You are making me look like a lunatic." I turned my head away from Lauren and whispered.

"No, I said, Lauren. My name is Lauren."

"Just doing my part," Cecylia said and laughed.

Natasha disappeared for a few minutes. I had no choice but to wait for her. We had plans to go to the Blue Moose Cafe together after our study group. She must have gone to the bathroom. I didn't mind waiting. Students left like cold honey dripping slowly off a spoon, lingering at the coffee and cookies. Ten minutes had gone by and Natasha was still nowhere to be found.

I settled into a plush yellow armchair while I waited. I was just glad the study group had gone relatively smoothly. I had only blurted one line of poetry. I hadn't gotten stabbed or anything and as far as I could tell, no one was under duress. Maybe. Maybe Aneta. I couldn't tell. But how long had it taken me to tell with Cecylia? Aneta had been gone for a couple of years. She could be fantastic at faking or she could be part of the whole human trafficking ring.

Natasha came down the stairs in a rush. "Let's get out of here," she said.

I couldn't tell if she was in a hurry or something happened upstairs.

She was halfway out the door when someone came up behind me and grabbed my elbow. "Hey," she said,

"I'm Aneta, the professor's assistant. He wants to talk to you in his study."

"I'll wait out here," Natasha said.

Aneta turned on her heel and walked towards the study. I followed and swallowed hard.

"Ah, Adelina," he said. He pulled out a pipe and stuck it in his mouth. He was taking this role seriously.

Professor Cohen motioned to a seat in front of his desk. Sitting on the chair's edge, I was ready to bolt if necessary.

"I see your new little Middle Eastern friend is taking the rap for the shooting. Terrible, these terrorist attacks."

I wasn't sure what to say. So, I said nothing. I felt the chill of evil. I shuddered.

I stared at him.

"I see you are keeping your mouth shut. Good girl."

Again, I said nothing.

"As long as you are quiet, nothing will happen to your little family. For now. Before I leave this position, when I finish my important work here, I will kill you. That's what I came here for. Cecylia too. That's what this field trip was for. I stumbled upon an opportunity that was too good to ignore."

Cecylia yelled in my ear. I couldn't understand what she was saying. Aneta came to the door.

"You can show Adelina out," he said, cool as ice. As if he had just given me advice from a professor to a student.

My knees shook as I walked toward the door. He was going to kill me. And Cecylia. Obviously, she had heard. Since he threatened me, she has been talking nonstop.

Kill-cause the death of (a person, animal, or other living thing).

"I have, indeed, no abhorrence of danger, except in its absolute effect - in terror."[2]

Aneta and I arrived at the front door. I couldn't keep all of this straight. Could I stop the inevitable? I considered going back in and telling Ryszard to do away with me now so Mom, Dad, and my new siblings would be safe. Then, what about Cecylia? My hand was on the doorknob. I turned to look Aneta full in the face. Could I read her? Instead of meeting my gaze, she cast her eyes downward. She pushed a piece of paper into my hand before sprinting up the stairs.

Natasha sat on the ledge of the front porch.

"Ready?" she said a little too brightly. Was it too brightly because I had just been told I was going to be murdered soon or because she was faking it? I couldn't tell. It didn't matter. Not right now. Natasha's woes paled compared to mine. She felt frustrated because she wanted to leave. I was frustrated because the guy who was going to kill me was sitting inside this house and a girl I wanted to rescue may or may not be on his side. The note seemed to burn a hole in my hand, but I dare not open it until I was far, far away from this house.

"Yes, let's go to the Blue Reindeer!" I said.

"You mean Blue Moose," Natasha said with a giggle. We walked down the sidewalk toward the bridge that led to downtown Middleburg and to the Blue Moose.

I thought of the second definition of Kill.

Kill-put an end to or cause the failure or defeat of (something).

I focused on that part of the definition. At the present moment, I had no constraints. I had a full team supporting me. Cecylia had quieted down, but I knew she was there, informing the team about the threat. Sharing all the information she had. Not only that, but she had given me the tiniest of devices to plant at Ryszard's place. It was a camera and a listening device. I was counting on the fact that he thought I wasn't brave enough to defeat him. That I wouldn't be on the offensive. I was counting on his pride to be his weakness. Hopefully, it worked. While he threatened to kill me, I secretly placed the device in his office. He was so busy smiling and gloating over his supposed victory that he didn't notice.

I stuffed the paper in my pocket. I would wait until we left the Blue Moose and went our separate ways before reading the note. I couldn't risk anyone else seeing it.

Once we were seated at the Blue Moose and sipping our coffees, Natasha shared,"My mother became a Christian about a year ago. My Father and older brothers are Sunni Muslims. Ninety-six percent of Pakistan's population is Muslim."

"So, what does that mean for you?" I asked.

"What it means for my family is a lot of pressure. The rest of the family has isolated my mother. My brothers mistreat her, hoping to strong arm her return to Islam," she said. A tear slid down her cheek. "I hated to leave my mother behind, but I had to get away. I had to decide for myself."

"Decide what?"

"If I wanted to be a Christian like my mother or follow my father and brothers. I don't like what my brothers are doing right now. It's not right the way they treat my mother. It's not right… I'm confused."

I grabbed her hand and squeezed it. I understood what pressure and fear did. It tore you apart. Regarding God, I had my fair share of time avoiding him, so I couldn't pass judgment on her. I could be her friend. We ended our coffee session with a few laughs.

Before Anne picked me up, I had a moment. Natasha had left to go study. I sat at the table, watching the door for Anne and anyone who might watch me. I pulled out the note and unfolded it. It said one word.

HELP!

CHAPTER
EIGHT

THE RECESS

Anne and I arrived back home to find Sabilia, Father, and Kasia waiting for us. I could barely get in the door before Kasia was pulling on my arm.

"Come play with me!"

"Could we see the note?" Sabilia asked.

Father Raphael paced back and forth across the family room.

I handed Sabilia the note and said, "I'm going to play a game with Kasia. I will fill you in on everything."

With all this spying and schooling, I felt as if I had ignored Kasia for far too long. She was doing well with homeschooling and had made some friends at co-op, but I had been such a major part of her life for years. She still wore heart t-shirts, but had branched out to different colors and sweaters instead of just the same hoodie all the time. That was a gigantic step for her. After all that happened in her past, it was easy to forget she was just a little girl.

Kasia was already in the library with the doors open to the armoire where Mom kept the games.

"Boggle JUNIOR!" She said, whipping it onto the library table.

"Perfect," I said. "Let me get us a snack. I'll be back in a second."

I walked back into the kitchen and opened the fridge. I was looking for some snack options when Father Raphael grabbed my elbow. I jumped and knocked him in the chin. He should know better than to sneak up on me!

Here I found myself entangled in the underworld of human trafficking and now terrorism, with my future murder looming over me, I couldn't handle anything more at the moment. I just wanted to play a normal board game. Just for now, I wanted to forget everything else.

"Sorry, Father, reflex."

He stepped backward. "I'm sorry," he said, "I just can't wait any longer. Is she okay? Should we go after her?"

"Aneta is fine. Cecylia already told you everything I know. We can't rush in right now. I'm going to help her the safest way possible."

"I know. I know." He rubbed his hands together as if he were trying to ward off some sort of chill. It wasn't cold. It must be the same chill of evil that I felt when I was around Ryszard.

"Adelina, are you coming?" Kasia yelled from the other room. "I have the paper and pencils ready."

I grabbed a few apples and the slicer. "Yes, I'm coming! Just a sec. Grabbing our snack." I sliced the apples and got some peanut butter out of the pantry. While I scooped the peanut butter into small bowls and filled two small mason jars with water, I watched Father Raphael.

"Can I give you a piece of advice, Father?"

"Sure," he said.

"Whatever load of guilt you are carrying, you need to let go." I loaded the snack on a tray. "And you need to do what you tell me to do. Pray. Trust. God didn't bring you this far for nothing."

"What did he bring me this far for?" he said, running his hands through his hair.

"I have no idea. You're the priest. Ask Him yourself."

I picked up the tray and went into the library. Geez. I couldn't carry the priest's burdens and my own. Why was he turning to me? Sabilia and Mom locked themselves in Mom's office. They had taken coffee and no bake cookies with them. They would be a while.

I set the tray down on the table. Kasia shook the Boggle letters.

"Ready?" she said.

I was ready. I grabbed a sheet of paper and the timer. "Go!" she said.

I so needed this normalcy. I had been getting used to the flow of days with my family. Meals together, private family jokes, games and just, well, time shared. I didn't want it all to go away. I didn't like this survival game. I wanted to thrive and enjoy life. On the other hand, I couldn't let Aneta or any of those other girls suffer. If I could do something, I needed to do it.

"Times up!" Kasia yelled.

"How many words do you have? Read them."

The game was helpful for Kasia. She was learning new English words. She spoke it well because of her time with me, but she wasn't proficient in reading or writing it. I let her count two-letter words for points, even though it was against the rules.

The doorbell rang and Kasia ran to open the door.

"Wait," I said. I jumped up and joined her at the door. I peeked out the glass side panel. Irfan. What was he doing here? He was supposed to be in jail. Well, sort of.

I opened the door and pulled him in.

"What are you doing here? We can't have our neighbors think we are harboring a terrorist."

"Adelina, you made a joke," he laughed. I laughed too. It felt good to laugh. I took my hand off of his arm, conscious that I had left it there longer than needed.

Kasia just said, "I don't get it!"

"Who is it?" Father yelled from the kitchen.

"Irfan," I said.

"Oh, I'll make coffee."

"We're playing a game, Irfan. Want to play?" Kasia said. She wasn't ready to give up her time with me.

"Sure. Oh. Boggle. I rock word games," he said.

I was behind Kasia, shaking my head in the negative. We didn't rock this game. We made English words such as "no."

He ignored me and sat down and grabbed some paper. "Let me see your word list," he said. Kasia shoved it two inches under his eyes. He grabbed in and read a few words. "Hey, you rock this game too."

I breathed a sigh of relief. He got it. We played a few

rounds. He kept his word list short and under four letters per word. Kasia had him laughing hard once fell off his seat. Unfortunately, the stories he laughed the hardest at were about me.

"Remember the time you cut off Muchiek's hair?" Kasia said, and she laughed while holding on to her own pretty locks.

Irfan tilted his head and grinned. "Handy with scissors, check."

"He promised me a poetry book and didn't deliver." I said. The dreaded red climbed up my face.

"You forgot about the part when you kiss…." Kasia said. I put my hand over her mouth. She slithered out of my reach and fell on the floor in the fetal position, snort-laughing.

"Make sure you give Adelina a book when you promise one. Check." Irfan chuckled. His slender frame shook like a dried cornstalk in the wind.

Changing the tide of conversation, I said. "Aren't you under house arrest?"

"I was. I am under 'hotel arrest'."

"Then how did you get here?"

"Thing One and Thing Two."

"How did you know I called them that?" I said, feeling the familiar flush of embarrassment climb up my cheeks *again*.

"What? I didn't. That's what I call them. Did you know they are fraternal twins?"

So, I wasn't too far off. And we thought alike, Irfan and I. Nathaniel and I. Whew, it was hot in here.

"They are outside patrolling the property. Sabilia

says we are having some sort of big pow-wow here tonight about some new intel you collected today."

"Oh, the note." I said.

"Yep, and we are disguising it as a bonfire. Kind of cool, huh? Like the night we first met."

"Yes, and the first night you lied to me."

He put his hand to his heart and leaned his chair to the tipping point. "You hurt my heart."

"Marge doesn't like us leaning back in the chairs like that. Yeah, Adelina is pretty good at lying, too." Kasia said.

Irfan laughed. "You didn't tell me you were an agent, either."

I couldn't help but agree. "True."

The tension released from my shoulders. Father Raphael brought us some coffee and joined us for a few rounds of Boggle before we packed it back up. It was good to see him laughing. Some of his words put us to shame, but Kasia didn't mind. "Theology." "Catholic." I didn't know how he did it. Irfan kept his words small throughout. It made me happy that he adjusted for Kasia. She needed that.

Outside, Thing One and Thing Two built a fire in the firepit. Dad pulled his truck up, loaded with wood, and joined them. Mom was always telling Dad he loved the woods more than her. When he got home from work in the summer, he went to his berry plants and fruit trees before he came inside. He was the same with autumn fires, inside or out. He told me it was his de-stresser. I understood. I knew Mom did too. She just liked to tease him about it.

Mom and Sabilia came down from the office and

went into the kitchen. The rest of us joined and pitched in, gathering supplies for the bonfire. Water, chips, and the Hobo pouches Mom had prepared.

"You didn't have to do all of this," Sabilia said.

"Yes, I did. I needed to keep my hands busy. Besides, we can't have fake food. We need to make the bonfire gathering look real."

The FBI and Task Force had swept the house for bugs and cameras while we were at Red Squirrel Rock State Forest last evening. We all had new phones. Sabilia said we had to act quickly because Ryszard would know that we had de-bugged. I'm sure he knew that when he told me he was going to kill me. It didn't seem necessary that he listened in anymore. He knew my schedule, where I was at all times anyway. Same with my whole family.

Hours later, we all sat around the fire. We had resolved nothing. Nor had an actual plan in place, at least none that was any different from the last one. I was the bait. Keep going to class. Well, not exactly the bait, more like the fisherman. I needed to stay in contact with Aneta and figure out how to get her out. After I got her out, we would use her intel to take down the whole ring. Ryzard included. I felt better about that.

Irfan would be "released" tomorrow. The FBI decided he would not return to class. We wanted Ryszard and whomever he was working with to think he took the fall for the crime. Cecylia had leaked some fake footage that didn't show his face. The people needed a scapegoat for the time being. We could tell the actual truth later.

"I love being behind the scenes," Cecylia said. "You should see all the equipment they have. It's crazy. An entire room of computer screens."

I was glad that Cecylia was enjoying her new job. It wasn't stressing her as much as being in the field.

"Some cute agents too." She said with a giggle. "Hey, can I borrow some of your boots?"

Cecylia and I went inside, leaving everyone, including Irfan, out at the fire pit.

We combed through my closet. She borrowed a few things and chattered the whole time.

The doorbell rang. Who could it be this time? Was it someone we could trust? Irfan was down there, out in the open. He could slip into the woods if needed, but would he have time?

I ran down the stairs and jerked open the front door. "Natasha! Come in!"

"I need your help," she said. "I don't know what to do." She started crying right there on the front porch.

I looked over at the fire pit. Irfan stood looking at me. I waved him away. *Please read my mind*, I thought. Run into the woods before Natasha sees you! Act normal out there. Smile. Make S'mores. Stop looking like a task force and FBI agents. Mom caught my eye and took the cue.

"Let's all have S'mores!" she shoved dad in front of Irfan.

"Who is it?" Cecylia yelled.

"It's Natasha."

"Oh, bring her up! The more the merrier!"

Natasha wiped her eyes and followed me up the stairs. We spent the next hour talking about school, our plans, and clothes. Natasha laughed with us, but didn't seem willing to open up and tell me what she needed help with. I had no way of knowing if it was family trouble or something related to human trafficking or terrorism. I couldn't very well come out and say, "You can trust us. We're on a task force and plan to take your art professor down." So, I said nothing.

Maybe she would open up tomorrow on campus. We planned another Blue Moose coffee date after art class. That would mean we had to ride the PRT, a unique feature of RMU that I hadn't experienced. PRT stood for Personal Rapid Transit. It was a monorail that had *cars* that traveled on a rail with stops on every campus. It wasn't a train, nor a subway. I was pretty excited about riding it. I had a PRT card, issued to me when Mom signed me up at orientation. Since Anne dropped us off wherever Rob and I needed to go, there was no reason to ride it.

"Let's go make a S'more before you leave," Cecylia said. The task force and my family had moved into the family room. It seemed safe for us to go outside.

I texted Mom: *Going outside to make S'mores.*

She texted back: *Come to the kitchen and get the basket of supplies. Come alone.*

Cecylia and Natasha headed out the front door. I walked back to the kitchen.

Irfan stopped me. "What's she doing here?"

"I'm not sure. She said she had a problem. She has a

difficult family situation. I think she wanted to talk about it."

I turned to the group in the family room. "Not everyone is a threat. She's just a friend who needs someone to talk to!" They all seemed to inhale and exhale a sigh of relief as one organism.

"We're sorry, hon," Dad said. "We want you to have a normal life. Just be careful."

"I know, dad. I am a teenager. And there are some people who have normal lives, you know."

I grabbed the basket and Irfan followed me, two inches behind me. I could feel his breath on the top of my head. It blew my hair up into little fuzzy curls. I flattened it down. "YOU can't come!"

He stopped and froze. I turned and looked at him. He looked like a sad puppy. "Sorry, I'm so snippy. Listen, how do I explain this to you? This is the guy I like. He's not a terrorist. Just an FBI agent."

"You like me?" He grinned a lopsided grin and turned on his heel and swaggered back towards the kitchen.

Cecylia and Natasha were waiting with marshmallow sticks. We each made a S'more. Rob had left a bluetooth speaker on the picnic table. I started some music, and we just sat and listened to Audrey Assad. Anne had introduced me to her. She is a pleasant mix of some classical sounds and voice. It was soothing. The flames of the fire calmed me. I stared at them and the whole dark world seemed to go away. Light shone. Darkness abated.

"Holy, Holy, Holy
Holy, holy, holy

Lord, God Almighty
Early in the morning our song shall rise to Thee
Holy, holy, holy
Merciful and mighty
God in three persons blessed Trinity
Holy, holy, holy
Though the darkness hide Thee
Though the eye of sinful man thy glory may not see
Only Thou art holy; there is none beside Thee
Perfect in power, in love, and purity
Holy, holy, holy
Lord, God Almighty
All Thy works shall praise Thy name in earth and sky and sea
Holy, holy, holy
Merciful and mighty[1]
God in three persons blessed Trinity"

I joined the song, singing loudly. Next thing I knew, we three were singing, arms around each other's shoulders. Peace washed over me. There was goodness in this world. I had friends. I had a family. I would fight for those who didn't. I would be the voice for the voiceless. It differed from the autumn before when I ran in through woods, flying Kasia like a kite while running from Ryszard. Those days, I felt alone. So alone. "My sorrow —I could not awaken" I had quoted Poe's *Alone* so many times in that season of my life. Today, I tucked it away in my memory to join the new season. The season of obstacles that I didn't face alone. I faced them with family and new friends. And God. I had welcomed Him in. I was a reluctant traveler on the road to Christianity. Now, I walked willingly along the path that had been chosen for me. Natasha had told me of the division in her family. Her mother, Christian. Her father, Muslim. Maybe we could be that family away from home that she needed.

I looked at Cecylia first. I wasn't the kind of girl to sing out loud. I didn't have the confidence Cecylia did. She was smiling. Tears streamed down her cheeks. I turned my head to Natasha. She was doing the same. It made me feel better. I wasn't imagining the feeling. I felt salty tears seeping into my mouth. I grinned. The song ended.

"Well, aren't we a pretty picture?" Cecylia spoke first.

"That was pretty awesome, girls. Thank you," Natasha said, wiping her tears with her sleeve. "I need to get going."

She turned quickly and rushed to her car.

"Bye!" Cecylia and I said in unison.

"See you in class tomorrow!"

Cecylia and I sat back down. I was reluctant to let go of the emotion I experienced. At the moment, I didn't feel like going back inside to receive more questions or instructions. All I wanted was a stretch of solitude to gaze at the stars and feel the warmth of the fire. Leaning back in the adirondack chair, I soaked my soul in the night sky.

A Cloud withdrew from the Sky
Superior Glory be
But that Cloud and its Auxiliaries
Are forever lost to me
Had I but further scanned
Had I secured the Glow

In an Hermetic Memory
It had availed me now.
Never to pass the Angel
With a glance and a Bow
Till I am firm in Heaven[2]
Is my intention now.

I was learning to enjoy poetry in pleasant moments. Professor Wrobleski said I would, one day. He had said that one day, I would be on the other side of suffering and I would have fond moments with poetry. I understood I was still amid suffering. For the moment, that was okay. I also knew what I was going to do. It would end my life, but it would let my family and Cecylia live. I didn't want to share my plans and risk someone convincing me not to go through with them. I had to rescue Aneta first. Breathing deeply, I set the idea of keeping myself safe aside. Right now, a cloud has withdrawn from the sky. I would be firm in heaven soon and my intention now.

The front door opened and male voices floated across the yard. Thing One and Thing Two stepped out into the porch light. They shoved each other off the porch, insulting and goading one another on. Irfan stayed a couple of steps behind, a smart move to avoid getting caught in the middle of them.

"Leaving, Adelina, see you soon!" Thing One said, and they waved in unison. I couldn't help but imagine them as the twins from the illustrations in *Alice in Wonderland*. Both with boy's beanies on their heads, including tiny flags. I muffled a giggle.

"Bye," Cecylia said, and we both waved.

"Those are some good-looking guys," Cecylia said and then I couldn't help but giggle.

"What?" she said, "I can look."

At Dad's direction, they left the FBI SUV parked on a logging road in the woods. Thing One and Thing Two made their way down to the path. Irfan moved in my direction. I was glad. Saying goodbye with a wave didn't feel like enough. Why was that?

There was a sudden loud boom. Flames. The force sent debris into the air. A red and yellow ball of fire rose out of the woods. There is a constant ringing in my ears. The chair I was sitting on fell backwards. I looked around and saw Irfan sprinting towards me in slow motion. His lips were moving, but no sound was coming out. Then he was there, with his arms around me, helping me up.

"A car bomb," he mouthed and pointed towards the logging road in the woods.

CHAPTER
NINE

THE RUINATION

The smoke cleared. Thing One and Thing Two staggered up the hill. Thing One's head wound spurted a fountain of blood.

"The trees protected us," Thing Two said in explanation. I thought they were dead. It was such a glorious thing to see them alive.

Mom, Dad, Sabilia, Father, Anne, and Rob came running out of the house. Cecylia remained standing beside me. I stood up. My ears were still ringing. Minutes later there were lights of a helicopter and an ambulance. It was all so confusing. Things here in the states happened so quickly. Someone called or hit a button or something and "the host of heaven" (as Father said) descended on you. It was difficult for me to get used to the lights and sounds of the community, much less the overload of them here at my normally quiet home. I was glad everyone was okay. I just wished they would go home.

Dad led me inside. "You've had enough excitement for the day, huh?"

It was both a question and a statement. I couldn't figure out how Ryszard got to us. Wasn't he going to leave everyone else alone? Just kill me and Cecylia. I reconsidered. Right then, I decided I would not sacrifice myself if he was going to come after everyone, anyway. I was going to go after him and the entire organization. Everything had seemed to stall. "Get our ducks in a row." That's what Sabilia had said. I didn't care about the ducks anymore.

Dad had led me to my room. I took off my boots and got into bed. Irfan hovered in the doorway. "I'm glad you are okay," he said.

"Me too." I said quietly. " I need to be alone."

"No, you don't," Cecylia said. She pushed her pink-jacked self past Irfan. "Come in and shut the door. Or leave. Enough is enough. It's time to take this bastard down. Excuse my language."

Irfan entered and shut the door. He took a seat in my green plaid chair. Cecylia plopped on the bed and grabbed a pillow. "These adults are taking way too much time to take care of this. I know they want to play it safe. Ryszard doesn't play it safe. I mean, a bomb just went off in your backyard and they're all like, go to bed, Adelina."

"I'm in total agreement," I said, sitting up and gaining a second wind.

"I'm in," Irfan said.

"You can't go tell your FBI buddies what we are up to." Cecylia said. "I know Ryszard. He won't play by the rules."

Cecylia told Irfan her story. His eyes were sad and bewildered. I followed with my story.

"You guys have been through the ringer. Man."

The house was quiet now. The moon shone through the window.

"We need not only take him down," Cecylia said. "We need to take him out."

"And make sure you don't get charged with murder," Irfan warned. "Things are weird in this country. We have to be careful."

Just then, Dad came to the door.

"Okay, Irfan, you need to get going."

"I'm spending the night, Mr. Hunter," Cecylia explained.

"Sure," Dad said. "But Irfan isn't."

Irfan got up and made his way to the door. We didn't get to make a plan. We were too busy filling him in on our back story.

I guess we could fill him in tomorrow.

"Are you girls okay?" Dad asked before he closed the door.

"You have had an eventful week."

He didn't know half of it and I would not tell him that Cecylia and I were next on the list.

Mom brought us some hot tea. She sat with us for a few minutes. I could feel her watching me. As if she could read my thoughts. I didn't like that about my parents sometimes.

"Brian is fine, by the way. Just some surface wounds. The trees saved their lives," she said. "Dad and I don't want you to be a part of this anymore. It's getting too dangerous. We're planning a trip. We are going to go someplace till this all blows over."

"No offense, Mrs. Hunter, but these things don't blow over. They get worse. Ryszard gets more bold. That's his M.O.. His weakness is his pride."

"Yeah, Mom, this won't get pinned on him. You know that."

"I don't know that. The FBI took the parts of the bomb they could retrieve and are going to trace it, hopefully back to him."

"Yes, more waiting. More paperwork," I said. "Mom, wake up. He planted a bomb in our backyard. Right under our noses. Do you think he is going to play by some set of rules?"

The neighbors had come to the door and dad made up a story. That storyline wouldn't hold water if this continued. We needed to relocate for a while to keep our neighbors safe, if nothing else.

Mom sighed. "Well, we are going. Tomorrow. Tonight, we have agents stationed watching us."

"A lot of good that will do," Cecylia said.

"Girls, don't do anything stupid." She looked back and forth between us. She stood and left the room. Her shoulders slumped forward. I had brought this on her. On her family. My new family. I was destroying the family. I was just beginning to understand what family meant and I was responsible for ruining it.

Cecylia changed into PJs and brushed our teeth. She kept extras of everything at our house. Frick and Frack were out there somewhere. Our neighborhood was crawling with agents and body guards. Could they protect us?

We decided to sleep and start fresh with our plans in the morning.

The morning that followed had an uncanny sense of normalcy. In the kitchen, Dad and Mom drank coffee. Dad pulled the eggs out of the fridge. Mom grabbed the blender to make a smoothie. Complete opposites. Dad enjoyed sausage and eggs. Mom opted for spirulina and spinach.

"Good morning, Adelina, Cecylia. Would you like some breakfast?"

Weird. How could we eat breakfast? Sleep last night was full of nightmares that had come true. I dreamt of Ryszard's face, smiling while covered in blood and flames. I kicked the covers off a million times.

"I'll take a smoothie."

"Me too," Cecylia said.

We drank our smoothies. Dad's phone beeped. He picked it up. "They picked up Ryszard for questioning. Good."

"It won't stick," Cecylia said.

"Aren't we positive today?" Dad replied. He mussed her hair. She hated that so much. I loved it. I agreed with Cecylia, though. Ryszard possessed the smoothness of an oily serpent. He wouldn't stay in custody. He would have whoever was available at his beck and call assist him and be free before the day ended.

"You don't need to go to class today," Mom said. "You need to pack."

I smacked my smoothie down a little too hard and drops of green dotted the counter. "What?"

"Yes, no need to go," Dad said.

"But, I want to go. The T.A. will be teaching. Not Ryszard. And I want to go to the Blue Moose with Natasha."

I acted like a toddler having a fit, but this friend's coffee date stuff meant a lot to me. I planned to ride the PRT. I didn't want to miss that.

"I'll be with her," Rob said. He had joined us, fresh from the shower. His hair wet. Beads of water stuck to his neck. Cecylia stared at me.

It was impossible for me to interpret her face this time. She needed to use her words. She jerked a shoulder towards the library.

I followed. "We need a plan," she whispered. "Will Rob object?"

"I don't know," I said.

"You can thank me later. I take cash gifts and Starbucks gift cards." He appeared at my side and poked me with his elbow.

"What?" I said.

"You can go to class. Dad said. Plus, I gave the 'we should act normal' speech." Rob said as he swung open the French door to the library.

Anne flew from her room in a flutter of papers. She stuffed them in her backpack.

"Leaving in five for all going to campus."

I pulled Cecylia aside. "You do whatever you did the other day, the ear thing. We can finish our plans later. For now, they have Ryszard locked up."

The day greeted us with sunshine and the morning chill would soon fade away. I grabbed a light jacket, knowing I would stuff it in my backpack later. Rob and I squeezed into Anne's lime green VW bug and left for campus. Mom had agreed to pack for me. We planned on getting out of town as soon as we three got home. Cecylia drove off in her car, escorted by Frick and Frack for the Middleburg FBI site.

Natasha met me at the door of the Creative Arts Center.

"Hey," she said. "Still on for coffee afterwards?"

"Yep!" I said. *Afterwards, my parents are going to hide me away for the rest of my life,* I thought. Mom had found a cabin online and rented it. The cabin, owned by a Mennonite family, was tucked away up in the mountains near White Snow, a ski resort. The cabin had a more remote location than the ski resort which satisfied mom and dad. I intended to savor the day while I had the chance and attempt to disregard all the unpleasant stuff happening- only for a couple of hours. Following that, Cecylia and I would devise a plan with Irfan to defeat Ryszard.

The sun hung in the autumn sky like a beacon of hope. This was going to be a great day. Class was amazing. The extent of information my brain could absorb when there wasn't a human trafficker teaching astounded me. The T.A. had taken over. Her energy was contagious. I wished for her to become the regular teacher and for Ryszard to never come back. I imagined the world without him in it. Maybe he wouldn't get released. Maybe they could connect the previous night's bombing to him. Authorities would bring charges against him for the terrorist attack. Bombing an FBI SUV should put him away for a long time.

After class, Natasha and I headed out into the sunshine. I stuffed my jacket into my backpack. As soon as we got outside the C.A.C., she said she needed to go back in and go to the bathroom.

"Okay, I'll be right here." I said.

Rob joined me, swooshing through the doors like he owned the place.

"I'm ready," he said. Two giggling girls gripped his arms, one on each side. These were fresh girls, not the same intelligence-deficient girls from the other day.

"You're not going." I said and stomped my foot. "This is my coffee date. My day to pretend I'm normal."

"Mom's orders."

I glared at him. I could not vocalize the dictionary words that came to mind without being chastised.

"Tell you what," he said. "I'll maintain a safe distance. Sit at a different table and all of that. Besides, I have Courtney and Raylee to keep me company."

They both giggled at the same time and smiled up at him. What type of girls attended school here? Idiots.

I was seething. I tried to shove it aside, but it kept boiling up in me. I had brought down a human trafficking ring and now Mom thought my harebrained brother, whose company had a combined IQ of one hundred, needed to watch out for me. Okay, so I got stabbed. He had no clue what real danger was. SUVs that exploded in the woods and agents only received minor bullet wounds differed completely from encountering Ryszard. Where was Natasha? She was taking forever. I wanted to run to the Engineering PRT station and hop on a car with Natasha and leave Rob in the dust.

Natasha finally joined us. Her face flushed. Why

didn't she remove her jacket? Maybe the flush means she is excited.

"Take your jacket off, Natasha. It's super nice out." I suggested.

"Nah, I want to keep it on."

Oh well, she may have a cold-blooded nature. Mom declared herself as a reptile and wore a sweater while others opted for a t-shirt. So, I left it alone.

I took off up the hill towards the PRT station. Checking behind me to ensure that Rob was following from a distance. He didn't. He stood behind us. However, there were also around twelve other people. I guess I needed to leave it alone and focus on chatting with Natasha.

"So what kind of coffee are you getting?" I asked.

"I'm not sure," she said. "What about you?"

"Hmmmm. Something with a shot of espresso. Do they have espresso shots at the Blue Moose?"

"I think so," she said.

She was so adamant about this outing, but now she seemed distracted and disinterested. Maybe she had heard about the SUV blowing up and thought I was in danger.

"I had to convince Mom and Dad to let me come to class today." I said, testing the waters.

"You mean because of the FBI SUV blowing up?"

"Yeah. That."

We arrived at the station. We passed through the turnstile after swiping our cards. Twenty of us were waiting when a car opened. Natasha took the lead and pulled me in with her.

"There's more room," she kept saying.

More people piled on. Twenty people. I developed an instant dislike for the PRT. I had pictured myself enjoying the ride with six people in the car. Instead I felt packed in like tuna in a can. This is not my idea of fun.

I glanced at Rob.It didn't seem to bother him. The girls leaned against him on either side as he grasped a pole. He grinned. That annoying lopsided grin guys wear around girls. Like the one Irfan wears around me. YIKES. Not going there right now. There was something that bothered me more than the tuna can PRT car. What was it?

Something Natasha said. "FBI SUV." Wait. How would she know that? They hadn't made that information public yet. My mind turned to darker thoughts. Why had she come over last night? Did she ever go missing without explanation? I shivered. Did she plant the bomb? And arrange that I go for coffee? Why? She was my friend. What did she intend to do? I gave her a quick side-glance. Perspiration beaded on her face and neck. All the color drained from her face. Her skin changed from a dark coffee color to heavy cream. Her mouth quivered. Was she on the verge of tears?

I stared at Rob. When he caught my eye, I swung my head towards her. He looked. His face registered something. Shock? Revelation?

A book of revelation came to me all at once. An epiphany of deathly proportions.

"Natasha, what are you doing?" I whispered. The pieces were all fitting together. The tears at Professor Cohen's house. The conversation about her family situation at the Blue Moose. The appearance at our house. The SUV bomb. Her. She was the one! She was responsible! Once again, I had befriended the bad guy. Led astray by a kind word and attention. Rob made his way over, jostling the crowd that seemed like one giant amoeba. People glanced my way, watching him, while listening to music, and turning their gaze back to their screens. My hands trembled. My insides are hot jello, like the Kiesel served in the orphanage. I am pretty sure I had befriended a terrorist.

terrorist-a person who uses unlawful violence and intimidation, especially against civilians, in the pursuit of political aims.

Natasha's jacket gaped open for a millisecond displaying a device strapped to her chest. She is a suicide bomber. Boy, I had a knack for picking friends. I looked at Rob. He had seen it too. His face paled. The lopsided grin was gone, replaced by a look of terror. I had hoped his training would kick in.

"Neutral face," I hissed in his ear. He complied. How did we diffuse this situation without Natasha defusing the bomb?

"Natasha, you don't want to do this."

"They're going to kill my parents if I don't."

"They?"

"Professor Cohen. He said LeT would kill my family if I didn't."

LeT is a well-known terrorist organization. Great.

"We can help you."

"We?"

"Yes, Rob and I are part of a task force," I whispered in her ear. I watched her hands the whole time. If she activated the button, we were all doomed. They hung at her sides like stiff wooden arms.

"That's why he wants you dead?" she asked. She had a personal epiphany.

"Yes, I took down his sex trafficking ring in Poland. That's why he came here. To kill me. For revenge." I whispered. "Come on. I can help you. We can help you."

She started to give. I could sense it. Rob had inched his way over to the emergency stop button.

"Can you save my family?" She said it a little too loudly. Rob and I both nodded a yes, even though we did not know if it was possible or not. The only thing that came to mind was to ensure the safety of everyone in that car so that I could eliminate Ryszard. If I didn't, Rob would die and Mom and Dad were probably more attached to him than me, so I needed to save him.

The PRT paralleled the river. Now would be a good time to blow it up for fewer casualties. What was I thinking? No. Stop it. Stop it.

I yelled at Rob, "Stop the car!"

Natasha's jacket flew open as the car jerked to a stop. People tumbled forward over top of each other. Backpacks and books obeyed the laws of science, flying forward and then back. Earbuds flew out. When the situation settled, all attention shifted to Natasha. Raylea screamed. Others cried and begged for their lives.

Natasha spoke. "All your devices. Here. Now." Phones piled up in the middle of the dirty PRT floor. "Rob, pry open the door and throw them out." He and a bulky football player pried the doors open. Rob threw all the devices out. The football player jumped and took off running down the track. Wow! Brave dude.

"Go. Guys. All of you off," Natasha said. She had to

repeat it twice because some individuals wept so loudly they didn't hear. We humans are so weird. When faced with a life or death situation, we react as if the worst has already happened.

One by one, the passengers jumped. The situation tested the character of every student. Some pushed and got out first, hitting the track and running. The more morally astute waited and helped those who needed it. Rob stood on the ground and helped people gather their things.

Natasha and I remained until every passenger exited. "You're coming, right?"

"Yes," she said, "I can take the bomb off and leave it here. We need to run like, what is that saying, 'bats out of Hades.'" She gave a half smile.

"Your Mom is right, I mean about Christianity. Jesus loves you."

"I know," she said, a tear slipped down her cheek. "Islam is about being a slave, Christianity is about being a sister or brother."

"Yes, sister, it is."

"You go first. Rob is waiting."

I made my way to the door, stepped onto the track, and ran towards Rob. I slipped and fell and he picked me up. I dusted off my jeans and looked back toward the doors. They closed. The PRT moved. I ran after it, tears streaming down my face.

I screamed, "NOOOOO!"

Natasha's face pressed up against the glass at the back of the car. Her expression conveyed both terror and resignation. Her arm raised. She pushed the button. Darkness enveloped everything.

THE REPERCUSSION

My eyes feel gritty. I try to open them. Everything aches. My bones are on fire and weigh a thousand pounds. Something sharp is digging into my back. What had happened? What is wrong with me?

It comes back to me in snippets. The PRT. Natasha. Her face. The blast had knocked me backwards.

"Adelina," Rob's voice said, distorted as if he were at the opposite end of a tunnel. Gravel crunched. People running? Arms lifted me onto something flat and the world turned dark once more.

As I woke up and blinked at the fluorescent lights overhead, a feeling of familiarity washed over me. Crisp white sheets. I tried to sit up, a wave of nauseous swept over me. Really? Again? I inspected my arm. Alright, I didn't experience another stabbing, but my head definitely ached.

"Are you awake, honey?" Mom asked. Although the

lights and sheets felt the same as my hospital stay in Poland, having a mom was with me was new.

"We're here, honey," Dad said in a slightly choked voice.

"Yeah, all of us," Rob said. I turned my head to see. Anne, Rob, Laura, and Cecylia. Yep, all of them. Wow! Totally different scenario than my last stay in a hospital.

A nurse busied herself with checking my vitals. Because I was experiencing flashbacks to my hospital stay in Poland, I fully expected her to have purple hair, but she didn't.

"How are you doing, sweetie? You need to take it easy. You have a concussion. We are so glad to see you awake. We need you to try to stay awake, okay?"

She took my blood pressure and listened to my heart. "The doctor will be in soon." And she left.

I gingerly leaned on my side to look at my family.

"What happened?"

"A bomb," said Cecylia. "They seem to follow you."

"I remember the bomb. Natasha?"

"She's gone," Rob said, tears slipping down his cheek. "I thought she was going to jump off. To take that vest off."

"I did too." I sobbed. And I thought my head would burst with the pain and the sorrow.

"That's enough talk," Dad said. "We can rehash the details later."

Mom and Laura joined me on the bed, smoothing my hair. Patting my arms.

"I tried *Sob* to … save... her."

"We know. Take it easy, honey. You need to rest."

"Don't leave me here," I said.

"Of course, I'll stay," Mom said.

"Let's go get some food, guys," Dad said. "Could you eat something, Adelina?"

Suddenly, I realized I was hungry. "Yes, please." I wiped my tears away on the sheet and released a shuttered breath.

"I'm not leaving," Rob said. "Bring me something, please Dad."

"Dad," I said, "She was really my friend. She wasn't a terrorist. She wasn't."

I started sobbing again.

He came towards me and wrapped his arms around me gently, like a whisper.

"I know, honey. I know. Get some rest." He stood and turned. Not before I saw a tear dripping down his cheek.

What was this feeling? People are crying over me. Crowding into my room. Watching me. Hugging me? It was like a burst of heat on a frigid day.

I could hear dad out at the nurse's station.

"You need to give my girl something to help her rest."

"We don't want her to sleep, sir. She has a concussion."

"I'd like to speak to the doctor when I return."

People listened to Dad. He had that effect on people.

"I want to try to sit up a little, Mom." She came over and pushed the button. I found I could handle a slight incline.

"Rob, tell me. What happened?"

"You ran after the PRT when Natasha closed the doors. I yelled *for you* to stop. You yelled NO."

"Oh."

"Then the explosion. It was crazy. People running. Screaming. A giant fireball. Parts flying up in the air. That wasn't the worst of it."

"What was it?"

"Seeing your body fly through the air and slam into the gravel. I thought you were dead. I thought you were dead." His shoulders hunched forward. He put his hands over his face.

"I'm okay, Rob." I said.

"All that training. I thought I was some big shot. And when I saw you…"

"It's okay, Rob. You did all the right things." I was so familiar with the things he was feeling right now. "You saved all those people. Without you, they would be dead."

I hadn't told them the whole story about Natasha. That would be an extra burden right now. I didn't want to overload him. I thought of Daria. I had saved her in body, but the soul scars were still being worked out, little by little. She writes me emails often now. It made me feel better knowing she had a family and a good therapist. My journey- my reluctant fight against evil was because of her. Natasha was just another Daria. Another Cecylia. I knew Cecylia cracked jokes because it helped her cope. The more frightened she was, the more flippant she became. I used to hate that about her. Now, I love it. It meant she cared.

Dad returned with hamburgers and fries. The doctor had given me approval to eat. I had to stay in the hospital for observation. I had no broken bones. No internal bleeding. Just some nasty cuts on the back of my head and a concussion, which was the more serious part. The other students had gotten away with only minor wounds and scratches. One girl had broken her arm because she slipped and fell while running.

While we were eating, Thing One and Thing Two came in.

"Adelina, how are you doing?" Thing One asked.

"I'm okay."

"Well, I have some bad news for you. You're going to have to be dead."

"What?!" I said. I looked at Mom and Dad. They didn't seem shocked or surprised.

"Yes, Natasha's job was to carry out a suicide bombing and kill you at the same time."

"Right," I said.

"Well, in order for Ryszard to think that she succeeded, you have to play dead until we take him down."

"Oh." I said quietly.

"We are sending you away. You and your family. After the funeral, of course."

"Of course." Of course, what was I saying? My funeral. Hiding away. For how long?

"We've arranged for the papers to say that Natasha and an unidentified student were killed in the blast. Some football player is claiming that he saved everyone. We're going to let him, so Rob isn't in the spotlight."

"You mean the one who ran away?" Rob said. "The jerk who was only worried about his own skin?"

"Yes, that one."

"Give me his name," Cecylia said, "I can mess with

his social media and put him on my 'do not date list'."
She batted her eyes at Thing One.

"We'd rather you not mess with his social media." He swallowed hard.

She laughed and put both hands in the air in surrender.

"Okay. Okay."

So, while the rest of the team took down Ryszard, I would be hidden away in a cabin. Just when my life seemed to be taking a turn for the better, he came back into my life and messed it all up again. This time, he killed my friend. I wouldn't let that go. I needed to talk to Rob, Irfan, and Cecylia alone.

How was I going to accomplish that? They planned on whisking me from here to a remote cabin in the next day or so. I wasn't allowed to leave the room. I was incapable of doing anything without help. My head throbbed. I just wanted to go to sleep. And kill Ryszard. I needed to talk to the priest. Is it considered murder if someone kills a human trafficker who is supplying girls to sex traffickers and terrorist groups?

The nurse came in and gave me some pain meds. "This should help with your headache. Are your ears ringing? No? Not since last night?"

"Well," what did I say? You *mean since yesterday's bomb?*

"It's okay," Thing One said. "She's one of us. We brought her here to look after you."

"Oh. No. Not ringing."

The agents seemed to be present and absent simultaneously. How is it that despite having so many people, they were unable to stop or anticipate a terrorist plot?

And did Thing Two ever speak? My patience wore thin as people continued to enter my room.

"Okay, everyone out," Dad said. Could he read my mind?

"Is it possible for me to speak with Father Raphael?" I said to Dad. And as if God read my mind too- the priest, Sabilia, and Kasia appeared in the doorway.

Everyone else left and like a giant sandworm twisting in on itself, the new group entered my hospital room.

"Not too long," Dad said to the newcomers as he left. He patted Father on the shoulder.

Kasia was overjoyed to see me. She hadn't been told exactly what had happened. She was pretty street smart and would figure things out quickly, especially if she watched any news at all. I wasn't going to try to hide anything.

"You look pretty alive for a dead girl," Kasia said. She giggled.

Yep, she knew it all.

"Kasia, don't say that," Sabilia said. Kasia giggled again. "I don't lose things as often anymore, but I have never lost my life." She laughed harder, like it was the funniest joke ever.

I couldn't help it. I giggled. "Oh, my head, don't make me laugh!" I said.

"Well, this twist caught us off guard," Sabilia said matter-of-factly. She smoothed her skirt and sat down.

"Yes, I was so broken up about Aneta that I wasn't paying attention. I'm sorry, Adelina," Father said.

"I know. It's hard. We're going to get her back. Meanwhile, I need you."

I leaned back and my whole body suddenly felt tired. Too tired to talk. Too tired to move. The nurse stuck her head in the door. "Those meds should be kicking in. Try not to fall asleep."

"What?" I wanted to sleep.

"I know! Let's play a game!" Kasia said.

"Great idea." Sabilia said.

Kasia pulled Boggle out of her backpack. We played for an hour. While we played, I did a lot of thinking about a lot of stuff I was unable to say out loud.

A flurry of activity occurred outside the door. Voices. Racing up and down the hall. Thing One stuck his head in the door.

"We got her. We got Aneta."

Father Raphael dropped his pencil and paper. He stood unsteadily. Sabilia was already at the door. She turned and looked at me.

"You did it again, Adelina."

I didn't feel as though I had done anything right. Father made his way to the door, and they both slipped out into the hallway.

"I guess it's just you and me," Kasia said. "They will probably be gone a long time. Aneta has been lost. You found her, right? You're good at finding things."

"Thanks, Kasia. Hey, go see if Thing One is still in the hallway?"

"Who?"

"The agent who left."

"Okay."

Kasia came back thirty seconds later with Thing One.

"Can you tell me what happened?" I asked.

"Sure. It was pretty straight forward. An easy op. With Ryszard in custody for questioning, we just went to his home."

"And you found Aneta?"

"Yep, and two other girls. All here. All getting debriefed and checked out. Only Aneta is talking right now and boy, is she talking."

"Good. I'm glad."

"This is because of you, Adelina, without you, none of this would have been possible."

"Yeah, she's good at finding things." Kasia chimed in.

"I wish people would stop saying that."

Thing One stopped and looked at me full in the face. "Survivor guilt. I get it."

"What?" I said and remembered Professor Wrobleski had tried to explain survivor guilt.

Survivor- a person who survives, especially a person remaining alive after an event in which others have died.

The professor had watched his mother succumb to depression and death in the ghetto during World War II. She couldn't come to terms with the fact that she couldn't feed her own children. The professor and his sister had to fend for themselves. When he finally made it to the United States with the help of his father and the Zabinskis, he suffered a period of survivor guilt. He didn't want to eat, drink, or participate in life.

He shared, "My father told me what a brave boy I was, and how I had saved my sister. My only thought was that I was unable to save my mother."

"How do you recover from survivor guilt?" I asked Thing One.

"That's a tough one," he said, straddling a chair. "I think you learn some coping skills. Also, you have to put it in perspective. One thing that helps me is to tell my story to someone."

"You too?" I said. "You have survivor guilt?"

"Yes, I've had it many times. In my-I mean our- line of work, we lose people."

"I guess that's true."

"And…"

"What?"

"Tell me your story," he said.

"Oh, right now?"

"Is this going to be boring? If it is, I'm going to find Mom." I'd forgotten Kasia was here.

"Let me walk you out there. I'll be right back, Adelina."

I formulated the version of my story I planned to share while he walked Kasia out. Should I start at the beginning of everything with Daria or just today? Was this the time for a watered-down version or the truth? It would be a relief to tell all of it.

It weighed on me. I couldn't exactly share it at homeschool co-op, like "Hey, did you know I'm an agent? I took down a sex-trafficking ring and stabbed the ring leader. Plus, I finished my English paper. How about you?"

At times, I had a sensation of being emotionally suppressed, even with Rob, Anne, and Laura. A feeling of relief washed over me when they learned the entire story, but when I mentioned it, a look of pity crossed their faces.

Laura hugged me and said, "I'm so sorry, honey" over and over, which part of me liked. Another part of me just wanted to talk about it. To be mad. To throw things. To say, "It's not fair or I want a do-over".

Today, I got a do-over, and I blew it again. I failed worse this time. At least last time, the girl I was trying to rescue survived. This time, I didn't even know who the victim was. I felt deceived, cheated and a failure, all at the same time.

The door opened, Irfan and Thing One came in. "I brought a guest. I hope you don't mind."

"Nope." I smiled and felt my cheeks get hot.

They both took a seat.

"Tell us everything. Start at the beginning. In Poland."

I breathed a sigh of relief. Everything. I suddenly remembered a quote from *The Horse and His Boy:*

"Child,' said the Lion, 'I am telling you your story, not hers. No one is told any story but their own."- C.S Lewis

I had asked Mom what it meant, and she had told me that we shouldn't share other people's stories, so as I told my story, I was careful not to share what I didn't need to about Cecylia's. It proved challenging, but I made an attempt.

Cecylia slipped back in halfway through my retelling.

"I came to keep you awake," she said. "But I see you already have company."

"Stay," I said. "Please stay."

We took turns telling parts of the story. Being aware of her perspective brought me solace, like a cozy blanket. I didn't feel as alone in my survivor's guilt. She cried with me.

When we finished, Thing One got a text and rose to leave.

"Thank you," I said. "You are right. It helps to tell my story."

"You're welcome. That was good practice, too. You'll have to tell the whole thing all over again to a committee at some point."

"Great."

He gave me an awkward hug and left.

"Good. Now we have a moment to plan." I said.

"What are we going to do?" Irfan asked.

"We're going to kill Ryszard at my funeral." I said.

CHAPTER
ELEVEN

THE REQUIEM

The experience of attending my funeral, well, the memorial service felt surreal. There was no body, so no casket. Just a jug of sorts with what supposedly held my remains. I camped out in the choir loft, hidden in the shadows. They set Ryszard free, exactly as I had foreseen. They did not have enough proof to keep him, yet. First, they said it was necessary to corroborate Aneta's story. None of that mattered. I was going to kill Ryszard today. The story would end there. Of course, I would go to jail. For the rest of my life. But my family would be free of me and the chains that bound me.

People trickled in from our church family, home-school co-op, followed by a bunch of college students I didn't recognize. They looked vaguely familiar. Oh, the football player taking credit for saving everyone. He looked sheepish, with his head down, following the rest of the students. The girl with the broken arm led the pack. Sadly, they really believed I was dead. I couldn't tell them otherwise. I hadn't expected such a large turnout for my funeral, of course, I hadn't expected to attend my funeral, either.

I had a small handgun in my backpack. I received training on how to use it. I couldn't use it today, though. Too many people, but I brought it just in case. In case what, I didn't know. Cecylia, Irfan, and I had another plan in place that involved no firearms. Because Ryszard thought I was dead, he would come in search of Cecylia. He had promised to kill us both. He would come.

A small band of press entered with cameras and bulky equipment. Father Raphael presided. He asked the press to wait until after he performed the service before they pounced on everyone with questions. He just said it in a nicer way.

Dad stood at the podium. "We hadn't had Adelina in our family for long. But it felt as if she had always been. She was the missing piece of the puzzle."

He got all choked up. His face was puffy from crying.

Mom jumped up and hurried to the podium. She patted Dad on the shoulder. "Adelina was brave. Yes. But she was more than brave. She was my daughter, so much like me, it had to be God. What a blessing she was." She couldn't continue. Instead, she stepped back from the podium to recompose herself and wipe her tears away.

What was happening inside my gut? Why were they saying those things? Was it true? Was this what family did? I didn't expect these feelings of security and trust to spring up in me. I was confused. This all felt so real. They really loved me. This was family?

Ryszard snaked in the back door. I could feel his cold evil permeating the air. I couldn't think straight. I was full of hate for him and love for my family all at the same time. He stood in the back, scanning the crowd. Irfan turned and glanced his way. I inched my way up to the edge of the choir loft and peeked over. Ryszard's face clouded with fury as he scanned the church, his eyes landing on the jug that held my "remains." A bloom of revelation blossomed into a wicked grin on his face. He looked straight up. At me. I ducked. It was too late. This wasn't part of the plan. This isn't the way it is supposed to go at all. His boots pounded up the wooden steps of the choir loft followed by a hush in the church. I stood. Frantically looking for a place to escape. I climbed onto the narrow balcony. Could I jump? We had such a brilliant plan. He would go for Cecylia. Irfan would come up behind him and plunge a syringe into his back full of a poison that would paralyze him within minutes. Before he went down, Cecylia and Irfan would "help him" to the basement. I would be waiting.

Of course, there were flaws in our plan. I hadn't counted on all the people. I also hadn't counted on the emotions. Camera flashes popped. People gasped as Ryszard grabbed me around the waist and flung me to the floor. Red carpet climbed into my nostrils. He pressed me down with his boot. The click of a gun echoed off the ceiling.

"You think you can fool me?" I couldn't answer. I couldn't catch a breath.

"First you and then everyone in here!"

The crowd below couldn't see me because of the partial wall. They could see Ryszard standing on me. People screamed.

A shot rang out. Was I dead? Something sticky and gooey dripped down my face and ran into my carpet-clogged nostrils.

Footsteps pounded up the choir loft stairs once again.

"Honey, I got you!" Dad said. The weight lifted. I sucked in a breath and looked to the right. The sticky gooey blood blurred my vision. Ryszard was beside me. Bleeding on the red carpet in a mushy puddle of death. Dad lifted me and hugged me.

"It's okay, honey, it's over. He can't hurt you anymore."

"How? What?"

Mom came out of nowhere and washed my face with a wipe.

Rob was there, too. "Father Raphael," he said. "He had a gun under his robe just in case."

I looked down at the altar. Press and agents surrounded father Raphael. He glanced my way and gave me a smile and a wave.

"Yeah, it all happened so fast, we weren't sure where it came from or who was shot," Rob said.

And par for the course, Cecylia appeared. "We totally thought it was you. Your hair is a mess, by the way. My advice, don't do any on-camera interviews."

"I don't plan to."

"Wait," something Ryszard said was coming back to me. "GET OUT!" I yelled. I ran over to the edge of the choir loft. "Everyone out!"

"What's going on?" Dad said as he grabbed me by the elbow and led me down the narrow circular stairs. He pushed me forward. I was going as fast as I was able without tripping.

"Dad, he said, first you and then everyone in here. He said he was going to kill everyone." I was breathing hard now. Adrenaline made me dizzy. Too much too fast made me feel as if I was going to pass out. I could feel the world blurring on the edges. No, I can't pass out. I can't pass out. I need to run. Run, body. Run. Dad dragged me through the double doors. Then he reached down and grabbed my legs and carried me like a baby out onto the cement portico.

He lurched forward. Debris flew in front of us, beside us, and must have knocked him in the back. He didn't stop running. We surged forward together. A blur of arms, legs, color, and screams. Heat and fear are pushing us. I felt as if we ran for miles. Finally, Dad put me down. I turned to look at the church two blocks away. Smoke billowed from the charred church, with flames engulfing the steeple. The church wasn't completely destroyed. It must have been a small bomb designed to hit the center of the sanctuary. Ryszard had wanted to kill the team, Father, Sabilia, Cecylia, and everyone. Did he even know Aneta was free? He must have. He must have known she would be here, too.

The street filled with people coming out of their houses, asking if we were okay. Sirens blared. Lights flashed.

I began searching for any injuries. Mom was already making her rounds, inspecting each person, embracing them, and quietly inquiring. The girl who had a broken arm was in tears. Mom guided her toward an ambulance. Paramedics took over and Mom found another person. I followed suit. Then Thing One grabbed my elbow, "We need to go!"

"What?"

"If Ryszard's plan fails, I'm sure his boss has a fail-safe. You aren't safe, especially if the media is sharing your photo, which they are."

An icy chill settled over me. I looked around for the rest of my family.

"What about them?"

"Yes, them too, but you and Cecylia are a priority."

Dad looked at me. He must have read the fear on my face. He guided Mom over to me. Rob, Anne, and Laura followed.

Cecylia came up behind me. "I guess this isn't over?" She said sarcastically. I looked her full in the face and I read the panic. I could read her so well now.

When would this be over? We loaded into two black vans with dark tinted windows. Laura phoned her husband, who planned to collect her and join us with the children. We hopped onto the highway and drove towards the mountains. We traveled past Red Squirrel Rock State Forest, the place where we met a few days ago. It seemed like two lifetimes ago. My body was shaking uncontrollably. Mom wrapped a blanket around me.

"I don't know how much more her body can take, honey," Mom said to Dad as if I weren't sitting between them.

"I thought I would feel better if he were dead," I whispered.

"I know, I know," Mom said. "It doesn't work that way."

"Is everyone okay?" Thing One said from the front of the van.

"Did anyone get injured from the blast?" Rob asked.

"Just minor injuries. Adelina, that was amazing work."

I didn't think so. Every time someone said that, I couldn't push the word *failure* out of my mind.

Failure-lack of success[1]

"That wasn't a failure, Adelina." Dad said. He had his arm around me. I leaned back into the crux of it. Did I say that out loud? Or did he read my mind?

"I was going to kill him."

"I know," said Mom.

"What?" I said. "How did you know?"

"I told them," Rob said. "I would not let you throw your whole life away on that piece of trash."

"We all knew," Thing One said. "Irfan told us. We gave him the sedating serum."

Irfan was in the other van. I would talk to him later.

"I don't understand." I said. I was crying now. "I wanted him dead."

"We know. And you don't understand. You were letting your feelings of revenge guide your actions. That's why we stepped in." Thing One said.

"Wait, don't you want revenge?"

"We want justice. It's a little different. We want to take down the whole human trafficking ring."

"I wanted revenge too, honey. I was prepared to kill Ryszard to protect you."

"Thanks, Dad." I said. Weird. I was sitting in an FBI van thanking my dad for being willing to kill for me.

I needed to sort all of this out. Family protected you? Even if they wanted revenge, too? Revenge didn't make you feel better?

"I will say this, Adelina, you are a great profiler. You knew Ryszard's weakness. You knew he would show up," Thing One said.

I needed to use his name. No, I liked Thing One better. Mom handed me a water bottle and a snack.

"Drink and eat. Then sleep. We have plenty of time to talk this through later." she said.

I ate the trail mix and sipped the water. Everyone was quiet now. Good, I could think. I thought of the Desmond Tutu quote Mom had on the bulletin board in the dining room. It was just a little scrap of paper she had cut out of a magazine.

"You don't choose your family. They are God's gift to you, as you are to them."

Instead of thinking about Ryszard and the church blowing up, my mind kept going to the things my family had said at my funeral and the things they had said just a few minutes ago. I expected them to be done with me. Like, we- don't-want -you-anymore-done. Like this-is- too-much-for-us-done. I had pushed the limits. I did it subconsciously, I think. Father Raphael had said that about the time I broke Mom's favorite piece kof Polish pottery. I was angry about something. I don't even remember what it was. I picked up the teapot and hurled it against the wall. As soon as I saw the fragments of blue and green bouncing off the wall I thought - Now *it will be over. They won't want me anymore. No one really wants me.*

Mom had said with sadness and clenched teeth, "People are more important than things, Adelina." Then she called the priest. By that time, I had run off into the woods. I sat down there by a giant oak, planning to go back to the orphanage, preparing myself for what was next.

What was next was nothing like I had imagined it. Father Raphael found me and sat down next to me. "Marge says you are having a rough day."

"Yeah, I guess." I said. I looked at the dead leaves under my feet. Those were me. Dead inside. Rotten. Worthless. I had a good thing going here, and now it was over.

Because I could not stop for Death –
He kindly stopped for me –
The Carriage held but just Ourselves –
And Immortality.

"Want to talk about it?" he said.

"Not really. I guess I need to pack."

"Why? Where are you going?"

"They will not want to keep me now. Not after that."

"If by they, you mean your family, then you are wrong. They are your family. Forever. For better or worse. They love you."

"I'm not sure I know what love is. I'm not very good at it."

"Sure you are. You are great at love. You loved Daria

so much you were willing to sacrifice your life for her. That's family."

"Oh." I remembered the feeling I had when Daria was missing. I would have done anything to get her back. "I guess I'm not that great about the day-to-day stuff."

"What made you so angry?"

"I don't remember. I just get so upset. I don't know why. I don't even know what I'm doing. Like that teapot was shattering, and I didn't know I had thrown it, which just made me madder."

"Have you been writing in your journal?"

"I was. I haven't for a couple of weeks."

"Could you start again? That seems to help regulate you."

"Yeah. I could."

We walked out of the woods and back up to the house together. Father had instructed me to tell Mom I was sorry and let it go. I could offer to pay for the teapot.

"Mom, I'm sorry."

"I forgive you, honey." She hugged me. That was it. She never brought it up again.

I went up to my room after that to process it. I wrote about it in my journal.

Family forgives.

When you get angry and throw things, family still loves you.

Weird.

I thought they would send me back.

Put my butt on a plane.

After that, I met with Father Raphael weekly. That helped.

My head felt heavy. I leaned on Mom's shoulder. I drifted in and out of sleep. My dreams were full of fire and interspersed with characters of Alice in Wonderland, the twins and the Queen of Hearts with Ryszard's face screaming "off with her head!"

My chin hit my chest, and I jerked awake. The van in front of us swerved and hit the guardrail, scraping alongside it until it righted.

"What's going on?" I asked.

"They blew a tire," Thing One said. "It's fine. He is an excellent driver. He'll get it righted." As soon as he said that, the van in front of us stabilized and stopped. We were on curvy mountain roads with not much room, so we stopped too.

"We can't stop here," Thing One said into a device. "Everyone get in this van. We need to move." Everyone in van one exited. We scooted and squished until everyone was in. The empty van in front of us exploded into a ball of fire.

CHAPTER
TWELVE

THE REVELATION

"Everyone out NOW!" Thing One and I yelled at the same time. We all hit the ground running towards the woods. Van two exploded behind us. The blast knocked us forward. I hit the dirt. Out of the corner of my eye, I saw the driver of van one running in the opposite direction.

Wasn't he supposed to be on our team? Help us? He pulled out his phone and called someone as he ran.

I looked around. Was anyone else paying attention? Thing One stood and helped me up. I pointed.

Thing One took off running. Irfan did too. Followed by Thing Two and the second van driver. Thing One tackled the runner. The other agents caught up with him and surrounded him. Dad, Mom, and Anne were at my side. I was glad that Laura had taken the kids separately. Mom must have had the same thought. She pulled out her phone and called her.

"Laura and the kids are okay. They made it to the cabin."

"Tell them to get out of there." I blurted. "If this guy is working for the traffickers, he was aware of our destination. He's a mole."

"Laura, get the kids back in the car and get out of there." Turns out, Laura and Daniel hadn't gotten out of the car yet. They turned around and headed out.

The agents had the mole on the ground and cuffed. Thing Two jerked him to his feet. Thing One grabbed his phone and smashed it with his boot.

We traveled down the road on foot to a spot where a helicopter could land and carry us to safety.

It seemed as if we were characters in a spy movie or something. As soon as we survived something, another disaster hit. We were pretty close to White Snow Resort. A helicopter had the ability to land there, so we headed in that direction. We had no luggage to slow us down. So, we walked pretty quickly.

"What's the plan?" Dad asked. He walked faster than anyone, including the agents. He was holding my hand. I was jogging.

"Well, first, we need to get you all of sight."

"Right. And then?"

"We need to interrogate the mole."

"We can do that on the way, can't we?" Dad said. "I mean, ask him what's going on. Obviously, he knows there's no future for him."

"Right," the mole said, speaking for the first time. "Don't call me the mole, I'm Bob. You've known me for years."

He looked back and forth between Thing One and Thing Two. "Now that my phone's gone, they can't track me or hear me."

"They? Track you? Hear you?"

"Yes, they. I never actually met the guy in charge. They took my daughter, guys. I didn't know what to do, so I listened."

"What were you supposed to do?" I asked.

"Kill you all. The vans both had bombs. I couldn't do it. That's why I blew a tire. I hoped you would read the signals. That they would believe the tire blowing was unintentional and not harm my daughter."

"Where is the phone?" Cecylia said. I guess she hadn't been paying attention to the smashing part.

Thing Two lifted a sandwich baggie with the phone in it.

"Give that to me," Cecylia said, grabbing it. "We can use this to our advantage if I can fix it."

"How?" Rob said, catching up with her.

"Well, do THEY know we are not dead?"

"Well, no," Bob said. "I would like to get my daughter back, too. If it were possible for you to repair my phone, they would be able to call me."

"I will fix it, but not until we are ready. Not until we have a plan in place. First, we need to cancel the helicopters. If we are dead, we can't be flying out of here."

"Right," Dad agreed. "Let's get some rooms at the resort and get some food. I'll rent the conference room."

Thing One canceled the helicopters. We rounded the bend to the resort. I tried to look touristy. I wished everyone wasn't lined up in a row. We looked like a task force. The only thing missing was music and a giant fan.

"Stop," Mom said. "We look like a task force. You guys, go to the ski shop two at a time, get some gear and change. Throw away your suits. We'll follow."

"Remember, look like tourists," Dad said.

"I can look like a ski bum," Rob said.

Dad, Mom, Irfan, Cecylia, Rob, and I proceeded into the shop next and discovered some clothes that would work. Mom bought some shampoo, toothbrushes, and other necessities. We went upstairs and got checked in. Once in our rooms, Thing One came by and collected our cell phones.

"Cecylia, we let your mom know you are okay. Sabilia, the priest, and Aneta are on their way in an unmarked vehicle."

"What about Laura, Daniel, and the kids?"

"We have them at another cabin further up the road. No need getting them mixed up in this."

"Good," Mom said.

"When's my computer coming?" Cecylia asked.

"It's on the way. Give it another half hour."

"Give me a place to work on this phone. And fast. They are going to be wondering why Bob hasn't checked in."

Mom, Cecylia, and I shared a room. Dad, Irfan, and Rob shared a room. Thing One and Thing Two had Bob and the other van driver.

I was hungry. I needed to process this. Cecylia left with Thing One to repair the phone. "Mom, can we go eat?" I asked.

"Yes, that's a great idea."

We walked down the stairs to the great room in the lodge. It was pretty empty. It wasn't prime season. There wasn't any snow on the ground. I guess it could go either way. We could either stick out like a sore thumb or people could just ignore us. A weird bunch of people who come to a ski resort when it's not ski season.

"You don't need to worry about being safe," Irfan said in my ear. Where did he come from? "Everyone here is an agent. I mean everyone."

Wow, that was fast. "Well, I don't mean to point fingers, but I have been bombed a few times with agents around me."

"Hey, I was only there for the shooting and, well... a few of the bombings."

I laughed. Why was that even funny?

We sat in the restaurant, Mom, Dad, Rob, Irfan and I. It felt like a family outing. Except for Irfan. I could pretend he was just my boyfriend. Yikes. I did like him. In the middle of this crazy, mixed up journey, I had really come to like him. I tried not to look at him. I knew if I did, he could read my mind, which said, *I like you, I like you. I like you.* So, I looked everywhere else. The menu. The lights over our heads. The artwork on the walls.

I ordered a hamburger without a bun and a salad.

"So, what's the plan, G Man?"

"Dad, no one says that any more!" Rob said.

"I'm not sure," Irfan said, "they don't tell me everything. Need to know basis, you know." He was looking at me. I could feel him looking at me.

"Well, I need to know. So after we eat, I'm going to that conference room to find out." Dad said.

It was such a strange feeling, sitting here, eating a meal after all we had survived today. I guess we were in shock. Or worse, we were getting used to everything blowing up around us. The professor had said that he got used to people dying, to sickness all around him and it became his new normal. Don't let the orphanage become your normal, he had told me. It's not normal. It's not how people live. People live in families with people who care about them. Here I was in a family with people who cared about me. I cared about them too. I didn't want them to die because of me. But it was nice to know they didn't want me to die, either. That sounded crazy. But, it was true.

We finished our burgers. Well, Dad inhaled his food like he usually did and watched the rest of us impatiently while we ate. Mom and I were only half way through our meals when Dad stood up and said, "I'm going to find out what's going on."

"Yeah, I need to get back, too." Irfan stood, walked to the counter, and grabbed a few bags of burgers. "For the rest of the crew," he said, holding up the bags and smiling at me.

I smiled back, "Uh, Mom, I'm going with Dad."

"Yeah, me too," said Rob.

"Alright," I'm going to the room. "I'll find us some fruit for later."

Mom always made sure we had the right food to eat, no matter what was going on. I walked down the hallway in between Irfan and Rob. It felt good to have them with me. I knew I could trust both of them. It felt less scary not knowing what was next with both of them on my side. When I had taken down Ryszard the first time, I felt so alone. I didn't trust anyone. I barely knew Marge and Jim then.

Ryszard. He was dead. It hadn't sunk in. Whoever he was working for was still intent on killing Cecylia and me for some reason. Everyone in my family, but why? Why did we matter? We didn't stop anything. We freed three girls. The PRT still blew up. What was so important about us? We were nobody in the big scheme of things. So, I said it out-loud.

"Why us?"

"What?" Irfan said.

"Why us? We're nobody. Who is going to all this trouble to kill me? To kill my family? I mean. We haven't done anything to anyone. We don't know who is behind this...." I trailed off for a moment. "Stop, guys. How well do you know Bob?"

"I don't really know him," Irfan said. "The twins know him."

"Does he *have* a daughter?" My mind was running a million miles a minute now.

"I don't know." Irfan said.

"Rob, go to the conference room and get Cecylia now. Bring her out here."

"What's going on?" Rob said.

"I think someone tricked us."

"What?" Rob and Irfan said in unison.

"Think about it. Has Bob said anything else about his daughter? Has he cried or even acted upset about the fact that THEY have her?"

"Well, no, but he's an agent."

"Even agents have feelings." I looked Irfan full in the face this time.

"Y...uhh, yeah, they do. I see what you're getting at." He squealed the last word, and turned tomato-red. I liked it.

Rob walked into the noisy conference room. Irfan and I stood out in the hallway. He was staring at the floor, his face still red.

"Adelina," he looked up. "You know I like you, right?"

"I do, but let's save that for after we are all safe, okay? Right now, we're not. At all."

Cecylia came out into the hall, flipping her hair. "Crazy in there. I need to talk to you, Adelina. Something doesn't add up."

"Not here." I said, motioning to a room across the hall. "In there."

The four of us went in and shut the door behind us.

"Get this," Cecylia said, "I got that phone working and there are no texts about a daughter being held hostage. No messages. No instructions. Nothing."

"Just what I thought." I paced the length of the rectangular table. I picked up my speed and ran around it three times.

"Adelina, slow down. What is it?" Rob asked. He grabbed my arm to stop me.

"He's not a mole. He's the THEY."

"The THEY?" Rob said.

"He's the puppet master. He's running the whole human trafficking ring. That's why the FBI couldn't make any progress."

"Oh," Cecylia said. Her lips stayed in an O as she jumped to her feet. "And the International Task Force is coming here. That was the threat that Bob couldn't risk. We just happen to be part of the team."

"So, what do we do?"

"We take them down," Irfan said. "All of them, before they kill all of us and then keep doing what they are doing."

"Cecylia, have you told them you got the phone working?"

"No," she said. "Something was too fishy."

"Go tell them it's a lost cause and do one of your girl fits, like, I'm going to my room, you guys are boring." Rob flipped his hair and pranced across the room in his best Cecylia imitation.

"Very funny, Rob. I can do that better than you." Cecylia flipped her hair.

"Then grab Dad and come back here." Rob said.

"What are you guys doing?" she asked.

"I'm going to intercept Father Raphael and Sabilia when they get here and make sure they don't go to the conference room." I said. "Irfan, can you go watch Bob?"

"Yep, I'm on it."

Fifteen minutes later, we had another room on the other side of the resort. Father, Sabilia, Dad, Cecylia, and Rob were all with me. We hatched a plan before Bob put his into action. While he was in the building, we felt safe. We didn't want to just leave or let him leave. Our mission was to bring down the ring.

"It is important for us to know who he is working

with. We need to get them to show their hand," Dad said.

"Right," Father said, "But how?"

Father and Sabilia had brought an entourage also, but they were a little more inconspicuous and had their team hiding in the woods and in nearby chalets. We had plenty of manpower. The problem was, most of them didn't know who the leader of the trafficking/terror organization was. And we didn't know how to get the rest of the human traffickers out of the woodwork. We could hold Bob, but we didn't know where he fit in the scheme of things. We were waiting for him to make a move. Any move. Like to use a laptop or phone to contact someone. Cecylia had that covered.

"What's the plan?" Dad said, He like to get down to business.

"We want to draw them out." Sabilia said. "We don't just want Bob or whoever he is."

"Right. But we don't want to die either," Rob said. "This is serious stuff."

"One thing we have on our side is that Bob thinks he is in control. He thinks he is running the show." Father said.

"Why is that a good thing?" I asked. "He may have someone setting a bomb under this place."

"Good point," said Mom. She had come in and closed the door behind her. "So, somehow, without everyone getting blown up, or Bob escaping, we need to get him to show his hand."

Cecylia slipped in, she put her hands on her hips, "Guys, you will not believe this!" She grinned and then flipped her hair.

"What?" we said in unison.

"Bob just used a laptop to message someone. I printed the whole conversation. I have it right here." She reached in her back pocket and pulled out a folded piece of computer paper. She handed it to Sabilia.

Bob: It's going just as planned.

Send a team and we will take this unit down. Business can resume as usual.

Vic: Team is on the way. Good work. Come on in.

Bob: Will do.

"Okay, now we can form a game plan. Cecylia, can you trace where this message came from?"

"I can try. I have to get the laptop."

"We need a team to follow Bob and the rest of us need to stage a greeting party."

Dad and Irfan went back to the conference room so as not to raise suspicion. Sabilia and Father made arrangements for their team to follow Bob and then joined them.

I wasn't sure what I was supposed to do, so I followed Mom to the coffee shop and got a cup of coffee with her.

"It's weird to just sit here, isn't it?" I asked.

"Not for me. I'm used to this part of it. I had to do this last time, remember?"

"Oh, yeah. It kind of seems anti-climatic, that's the right phrase, huh?"

"Yes, I'm sure for you it is, all the scary things

you've been through. This must just be, well… weird." Mom said.

"Exactly the word I was thinking." I said.

"We think alike. I'd rather you be here with me, anyway. I know you're safe." She said and smiled.

"Bring any good books?" Mom laughed. Books were always my go-to.

"Turns out, they had a few good ones in the gift shop." Mom pulled a few books out of her bag and handed me one.

So, this is what it was like. Family. We sat and read for an hour. Every once in a while, Mom looked up and said, "listen to this," and she read me a few lines.

I did the same. We went back and forth like this, sharing bits and pieces of our books as we did our lives. It felt good.

Dad and Rob joined us when the hour was winding down. "Bob's team sent here to eliminate us is in custody. They didn't even make it close to the resort. Sabilia's team got them all. Still waiting to hear about Bob. Hopefully, he led them to the heart of the operation."

"What are you reading?" Rob asked.

"The Hobbit," I said, holding up the book.

"I love that book! Especially the part where he says, 'I am looking for someone to share in an adventure that I am arranging, and it's very difficult to find anyone.'"

"Me too."

"Read that part," Dad said.

So I did.

"I am looking for someone to share in an adventure

that I am arranging, and it's very difficult to find anyone.'

I should think so — in these parts! We are plain quiet folk and have no use for adventures. Nasty disturbing uncomfortable things! Make you late for dinner!"

"Where can a girl find a good latte?" said Cecylia's voice from behind me.

"Let me get you something," Mom offered. "I think I know what you like."

Cecylia plopped down in a seat. "Well, we did it, guys. Bob led them right to the ring of human traffickers. Twenty people. Ten more girls were freed."

Irfan came sauntering in. "It's over guys. We got 'em," he said triumphantly.

I breathed a sigh of relief. A deep sigh. It was over. No more Ryszard. No more human trafficking ring in north central West Virginia. For some odd reason, tears streamed down my cheeks. Hot, salty tears. My shoulders convulsed. I dropped my book. Mom wrapped her arm around me.

"It's okay, honey. It's okay."

"You're just messing up your face," Cecylia said. "I mean, if reporters come to interview us for the news or something, I want to be camera ready."

"You always say the right thing, Cecylia," and we laughed.

A few hours later, we pulled into our driveway. Our house had never looked so beautiful. The porch lights were on. The white columns glowed in the moonlight.

"Um, Mrs. Hunter, do you mind if I spend the night?" Cecylia said as she got out of the SUV.

"Not at all, honey, you're family."

Family- a group consisting of parents and children living together in a household.

———

What to read next:

The Girl Who Was Blacklisted

NOTES

CHAPTER 2

1. Emily Dickinson, *"Why Do I Love You, Sir"*
2. Emily Dickinson, *"Why Do I Love You, Sir?"*
3. William Shakespeare, *Sonnet 137*

CHAPTER 3

1. C.S. Lewis, *The Case For Christianity*
2. Robert Frost, *"The Road Not Taken"*
3. Robert Frost, *"The Road Not Taken"*
4. Robert Frost, *"The Road Not Taken"*
5. Robert Frost, *"The Road Not Taken"*
6. Robert Frost, *"The Road Not Taken"*

CHAPTER 4

1. Emily Dickinson, *"A Death Blow Is A Life Blow To Some"*
2. Leonardo Da Vinci

CHAPTER 5

1. Edgar Allan Poe, *"Slience"*

CHAPTER 7

1. Ralph Waldo Emerson, *"Freedom"*
2. Edgar Allan Poe, *"The Fall of the House of Usher"*

CHAPTER 8

1. Reginald Heber
2. Emily Dickinson, *"A Cloud Withdrew From The Sky"*

CHAPTER 11

1. Emily Dickinon, *"Because I Could Not Stop For Death"*

ABOUT THE AUTHOR

Kathleen Guire is the mother of seven, four through adoption, former National Parent of the Year, author, teacher, and speaker. She loves connecting with readers through her website (Kathleenguireauthor.com).

For more information,
about Kathleen, check out her website and follow her on social
media!
www.kathleenguireauthor.com
kathleenguire@gmail.com
https://linktr.ee/kguire

ALSO BY KATHLEEN GUIRE

What to read next

The Girl Who Was Blacklisted

If you missed it, Grab

The Girl Who Didn't Exist

The Girl Who Was Trafficked